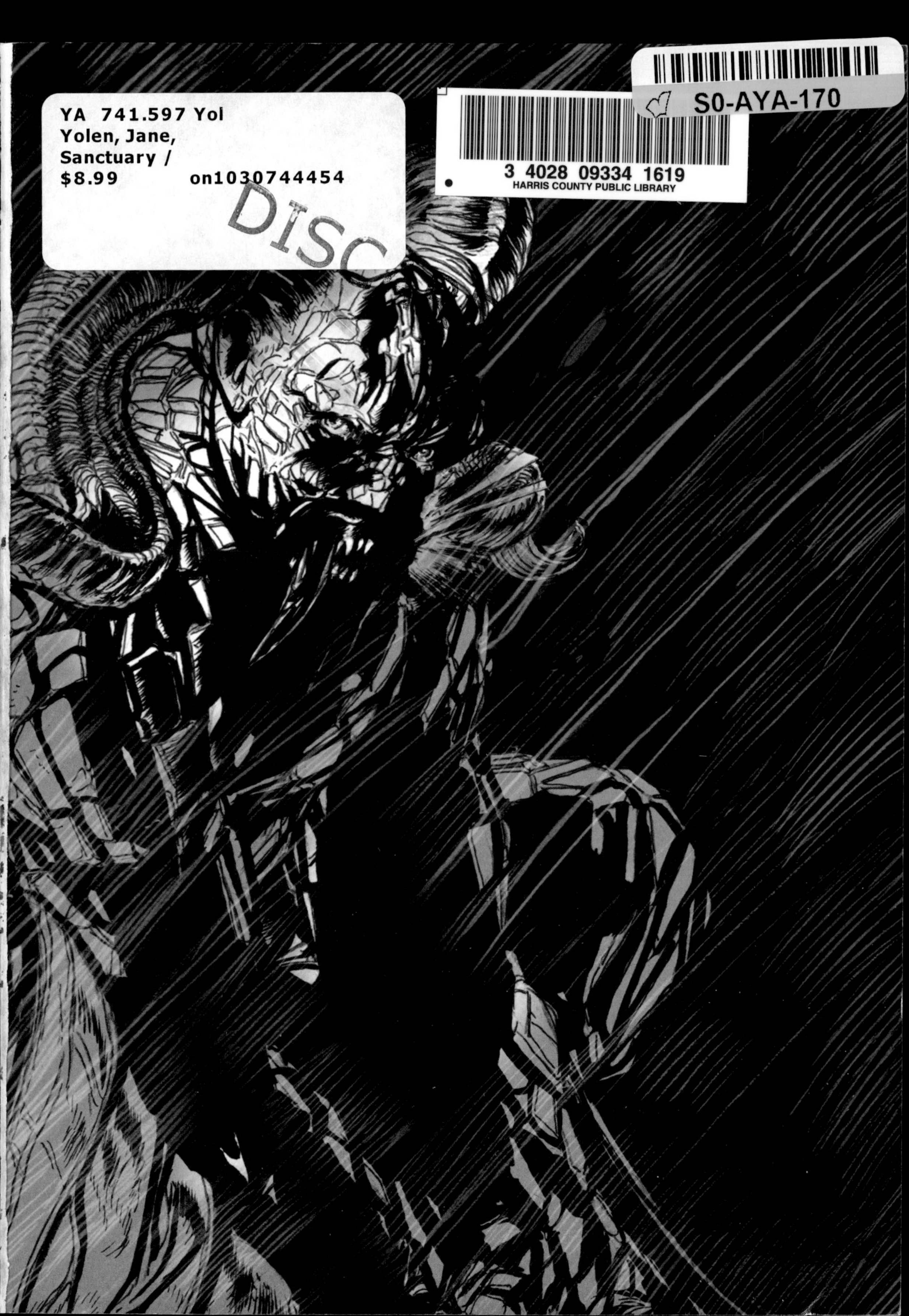

For David, who loves graphic novels and Scotland. —JY

For Ari, who's been bugging me to write this one from the
moment she finished the first. —AS

To my beautiful wife, Katie Zangara, who is the light of my life.
I love you. —OZ

Story by Jane Yolen and Adam Stemple
Illustrations by Orion Zangara
Lettering by Bill Hauser

Text copyright © 2018 by Jane Yolen and Adam Stemple
Art copyright © 2018 by Orion Zangara

Graphic Universe™ is a trademark of Lerner Publishing Group, Inc.

Graphic Universe™
A division of Lerner Publishing Group, Inc.
241 First Avenue North
Minneapolis, MN 55401 USA

For reading levels and more information, look up this title at www.lernerbooks.com.

Main body text set in CCWildWords 7/8. Typeface provided by Comicraft.

Library of Congress Cataloging-in-Publication Data

Names: Yolen, Jane, author. | Stemple, Adam, author. | Zangara, Orion, illustrator.
Title: Sanctuary / written by Jane Yolen and Adam Stemple ; illustrated by Orion Zangara.
Description: Minneapolis : Graphic Universe, [2018] | Series: The Stone Man mysteries ; book two
  | Summary: "When a mysterious young woman takes refuge within Silex's Edinburgh church, it
  brings supernatural trouble for the gargoyle and his assistant, Craig" —Provided by publisher.
  | Identifiers: LCCN 2017006471 (print) | LCCN 2017033758 (ebook) | ISBN 9781512498585
  (eb pdf) | ISBN 9781467741972 (lb : alk. paper) | ISBN 9781541510432 (pbk.)
Subjects: LCSH: Graphic novels. | CYAC: Graphic novels. | Gargoyles—Fiction. | Supernatural—
  Fiction. | Demonology—Fiction. | Scotland—History—20th century—Fiction. | Mystery and
  detective stories.
Classification: LCC PZ7.7.Y65 (ebook) | LCC PZ7.7.Y65 San 2018 (print) | DDC 741.5/973—dc23

LC record available at https://lccn.loc.gov/2017006471

Manufactured in the United States of America
1-36194-16978-10/6/2017

THE STONE MAN MYSTERIES

BOOK TWO

Sanctuary

JANE YOLEN AND ADAM STEMPLE
ILLUSTRATED BY ORION ZANGARA

GRAPHIC UNIVERSE™ • MINNEAPOLIS

Edinburgh, Scotland. The early 1930s. Young Craig, a desperate runaway, goes to the top of a church to throw himself off. But he is saved by a strange stone man, a gargoyle named Silex, who can move and speak but cannot leave the church parapet. Silex runs a detective agency and hires Craig to be his chief clue finder, since his last assistant has mysteriously disappeared and the church's priest, Father Harris, is getting too old and sick to help.

Shocked, yet happy to have important work to do, Craig signs on. Together, the gargoyle and the young lad solve the mysterious murder of an earl, as well as the deaths of several street people. But the solution points to a deeper, uglier scenario. One that involves freeing the Stone Man from his bonds, which will turn him from a force for good back into the evil demon he once was. In that form, he would threaten not only the church, Edinburgh, and Scotland, but indeed the entire world.

Silex doesn't want that. Craig doesn't want that. Father Harris dies to see that it can never happen. And yet the terror might well be starting up all over again.

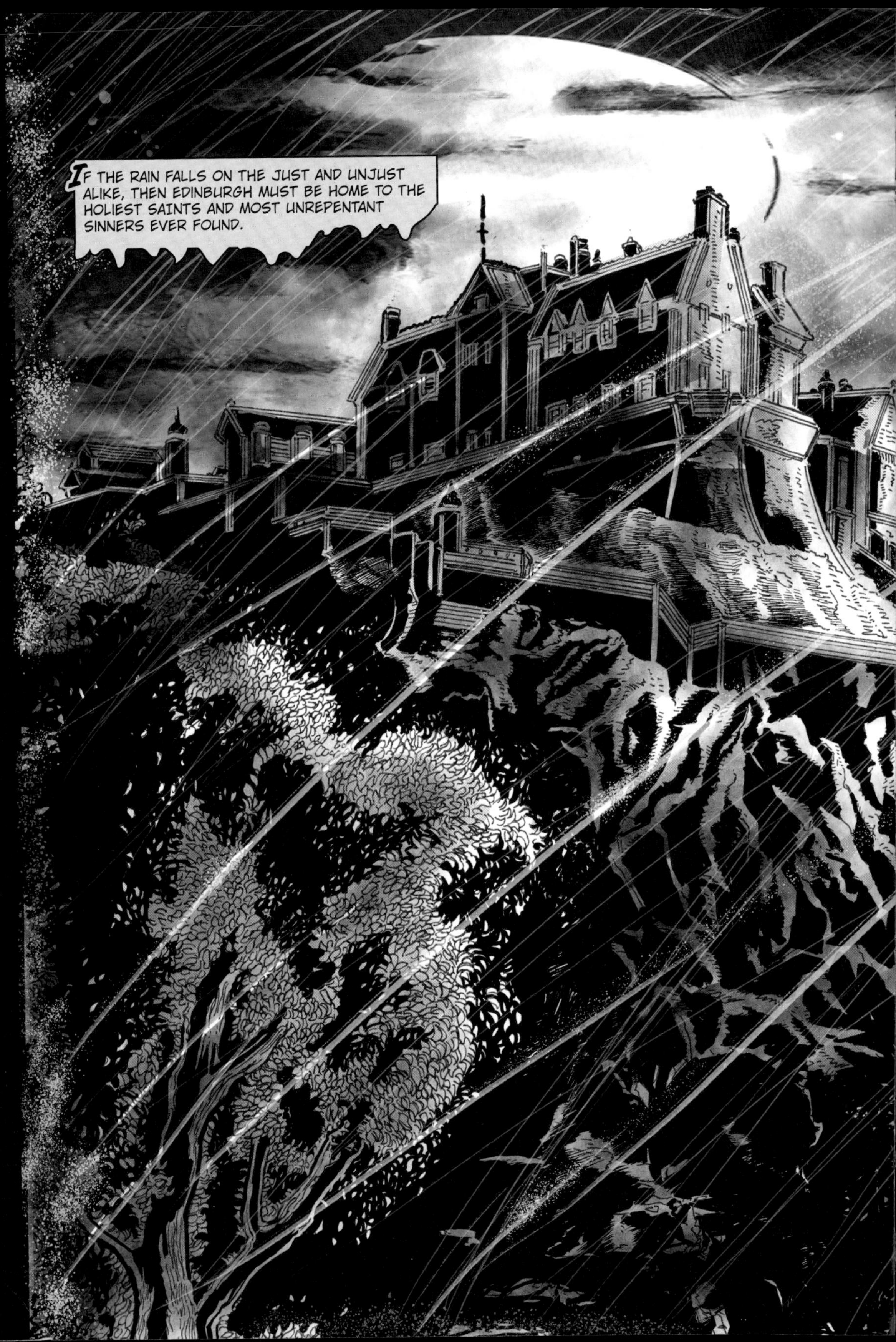
IF THE RAIN FALLS ON THE JUST AND UNJUST ALIKE, THEN EDINBURGH MUST BE HOME TO THE HOLIEST SAINTS AND MOST UNREPENTANT SINNERS EVER FOUND.

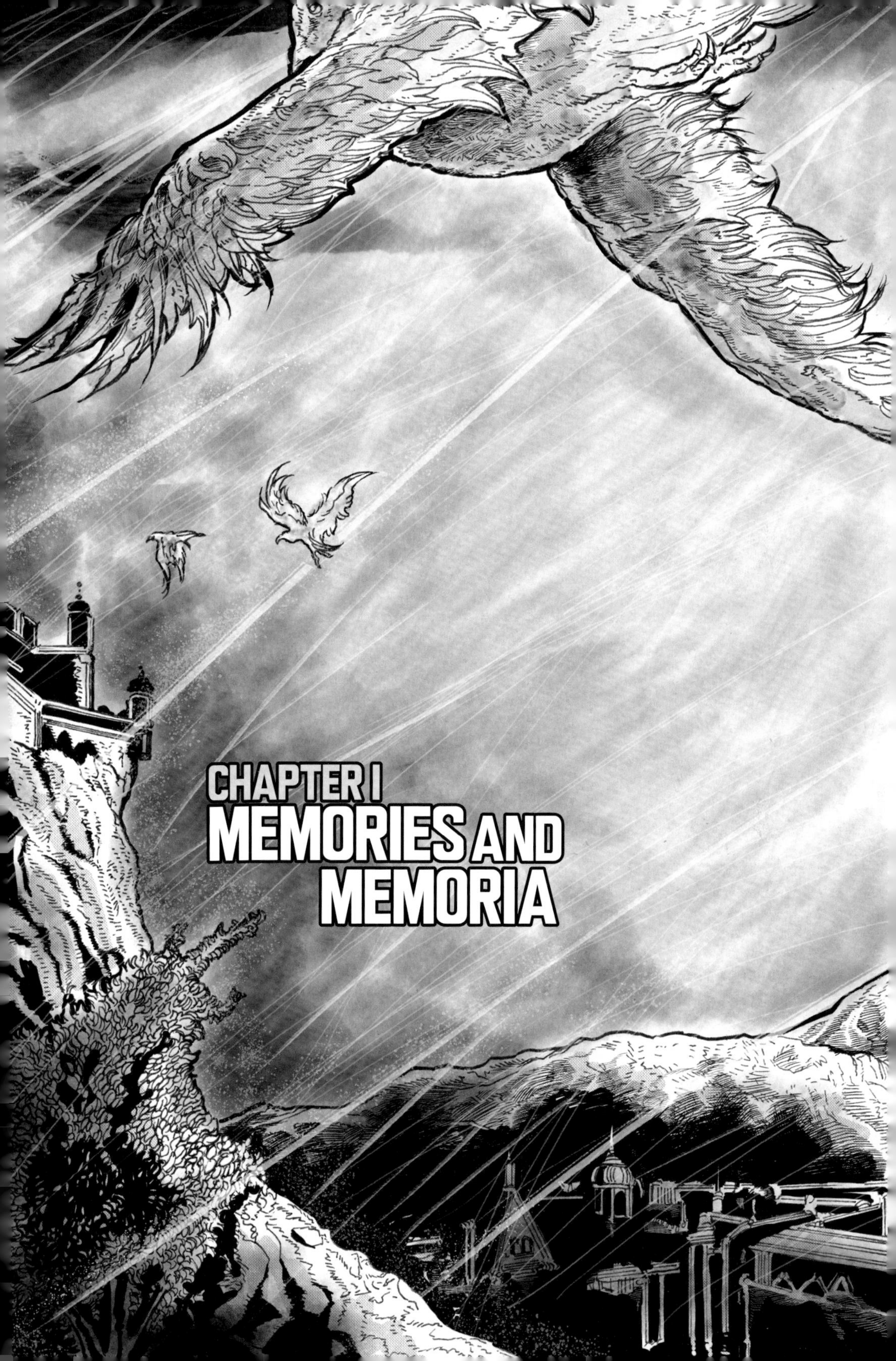
CHAPTER I
MEMORIES AND MEMORIA

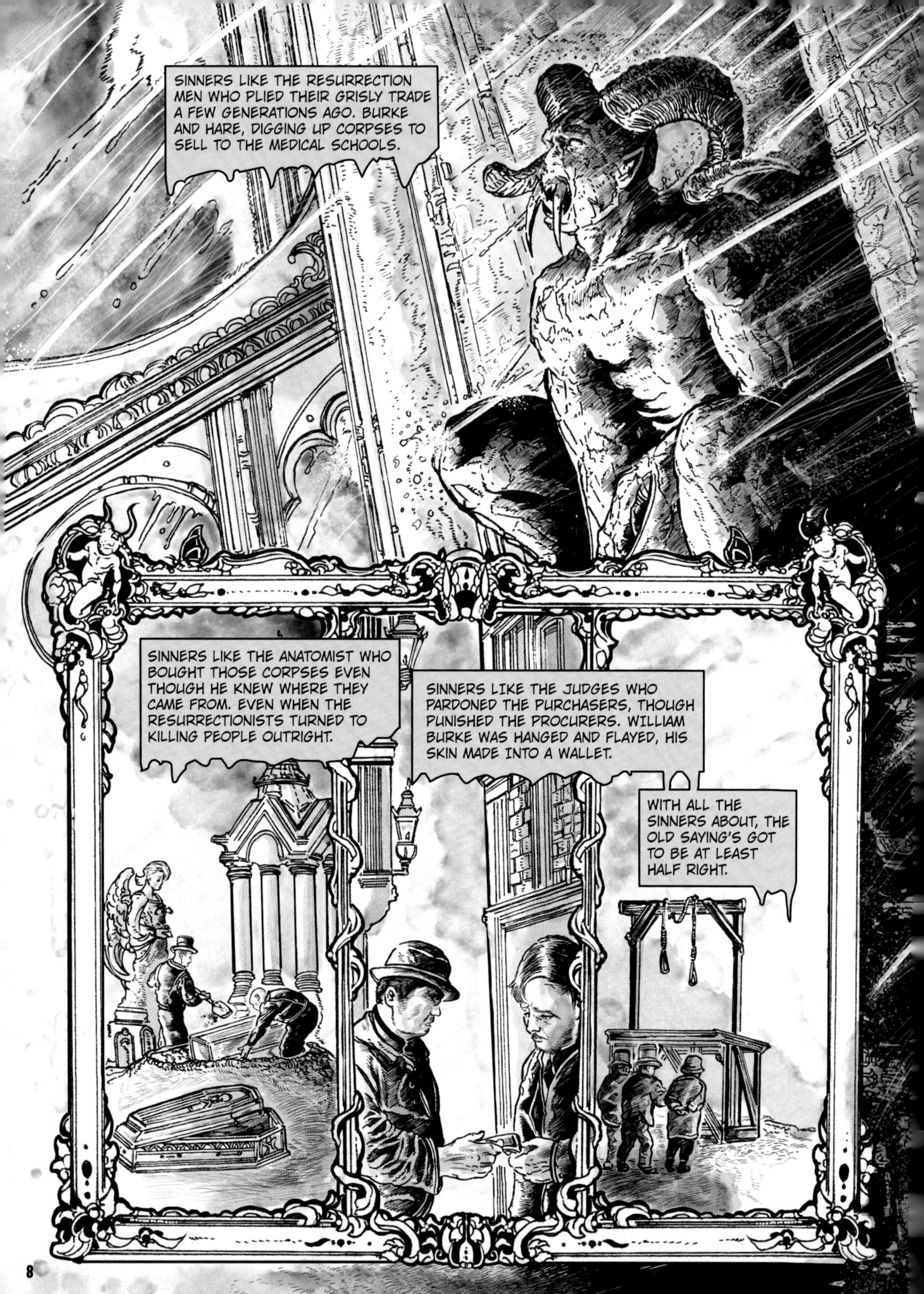
SINNERS LIKE THE RESURRECTION MEN WHO PLIED THEIR GRISLY TRADE A FEW GENERATIONS AGO. BURKE AND HARE, DIGGING UP CORPSES TO SELL TO THE MEDICAL SCHOOLS.
SINNERS LIKE THE ANATOMIST WHO BOUGHT THOSE CORPSES EVEN THOUGH HE KNEW WHERE THEY CAME FROM. EVEN WHEN THE RESURRECTIONISTS TURNED TO KILLING PEOPLE OUTRIGHT.
SINNERS LIKE THE JUDGES WHO PARDONED THE PURCHASERS, THOUGH PUNISHED THE PROCURERS. WILLIAM BURKE WAS HANGED AND FLAYED, HIS SKIN MADE INTO A WALLET.
WITH ALL THE SINNERS ABOUT, THE OLD SAYING'S GOT TO BE AT LEAST HALF RIGHT.

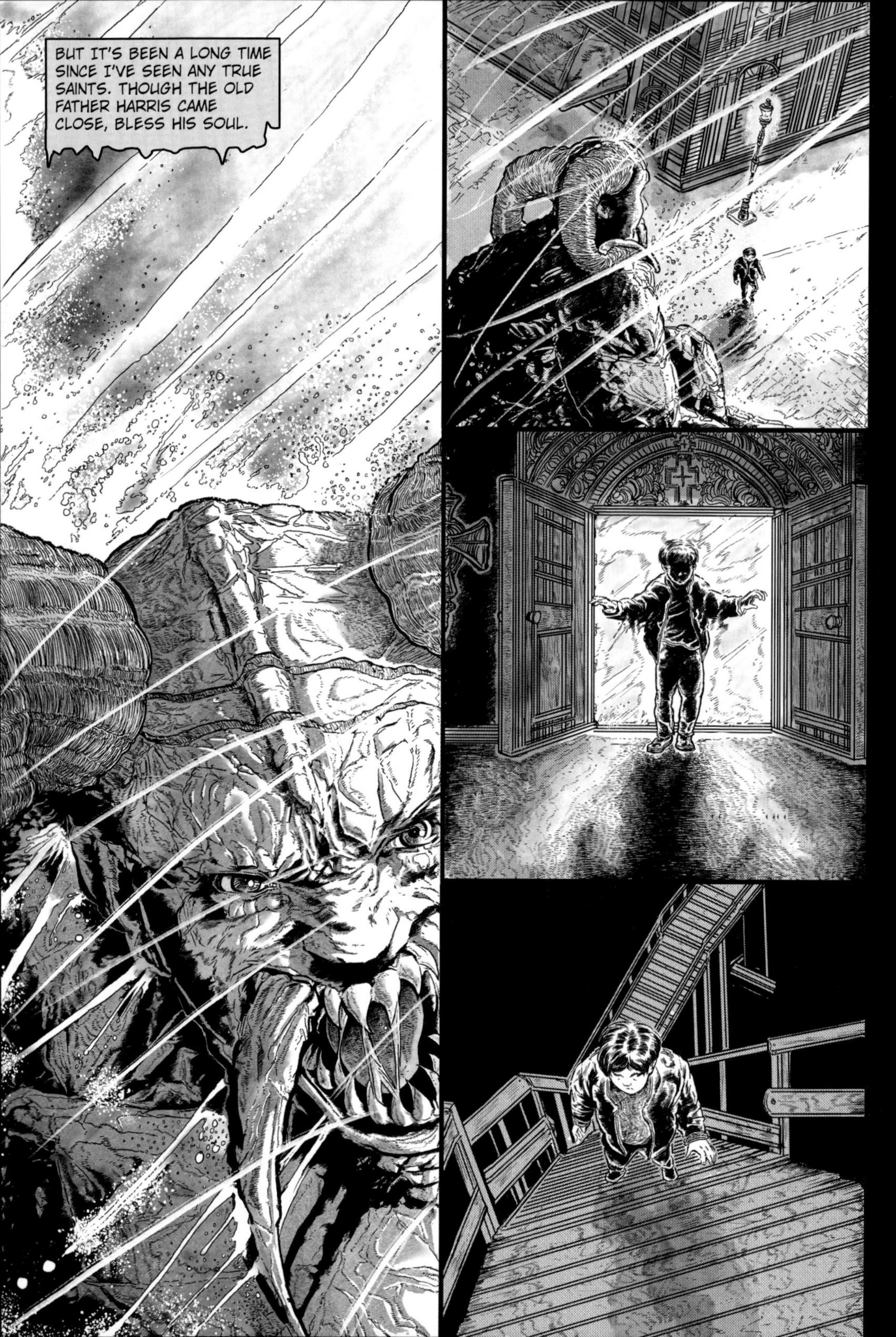
BUT IT'S BEEN A LONG TIME SINCE I'VE SEEN ANY TRUE SAINTS. THOUGH THE OLD FATHER HARRIS CAME CLOSE, BLESS HIS SOUL.

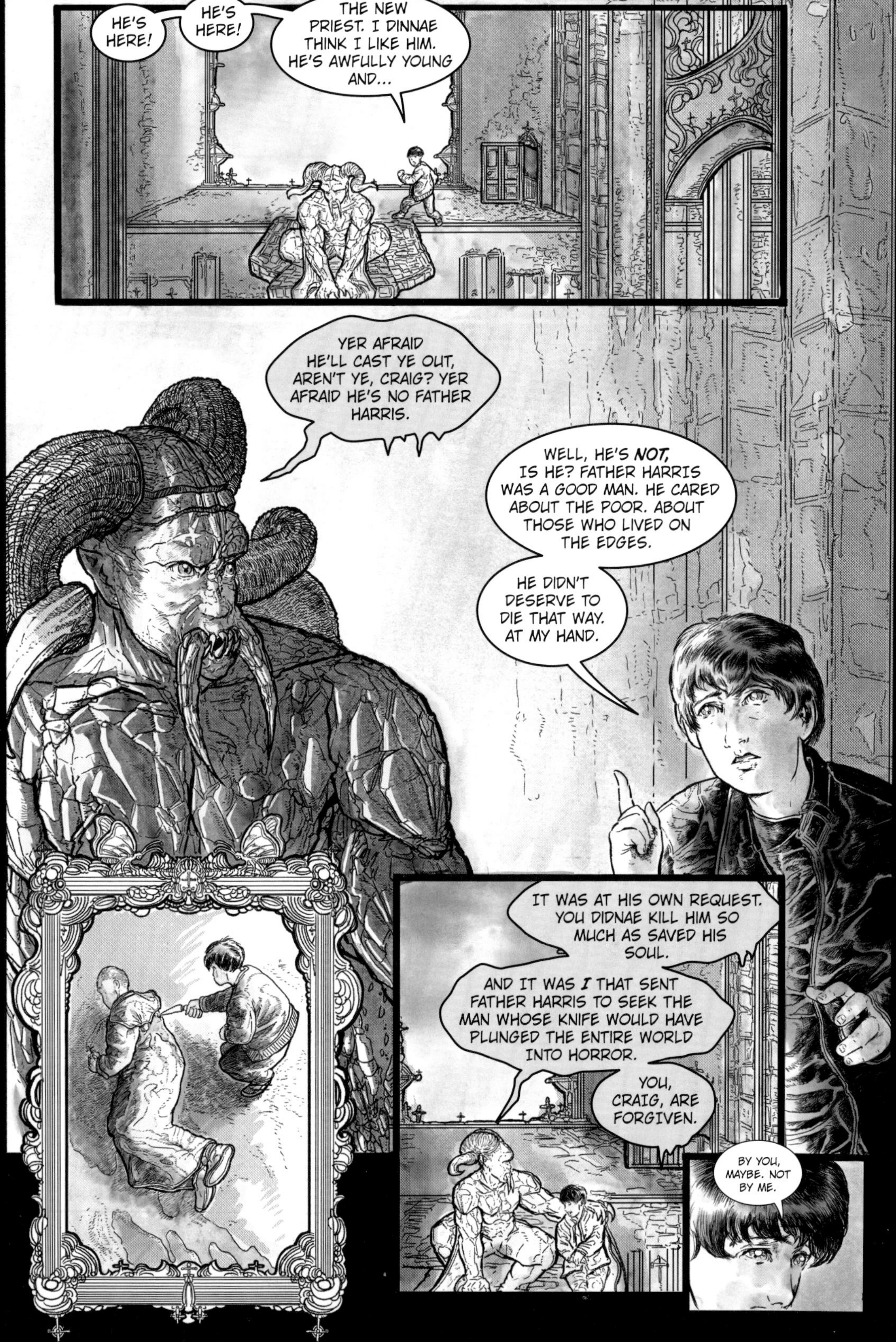
HE'S HERE!
HE'S HERE!
THE NEW PRIEST. I DINNAE THINK I LIKE HIM. HE'S AWFULLY YOUNG AND...
YER AFRAID HE'LL CAST YE OUT, AREN'T YE, CRAIG? YER AFRAID HE'S NO FATHER HARRIS.
WELL, HE'S *NOT,* IS HE? FATHER HARRIS WAS A GOOD MAN. HE CARED ABOUT THE POOR. ABOUT THOSE WHO LIVED ON THE EDGES.
HE DIDN'T DESERVE TO DIE THAT WAY. AT MY HAND.
IT WAS AT HIS OWN REQUEST. YOU DIDNAE KILL HIM SO MUCH AS SAVED HIS SOUL.
AND IT WAS *I* THAT SENT FATHER HARRIS TO SEEK THE MAN WHOSE KNIFE WOULD HAVE PLUNGED THE ENTIRE WORLD INTO HORROR.
YOU, CRAIG, ARE FORGIVEN.
BY YOU, MAYBE. NOT BY ME.

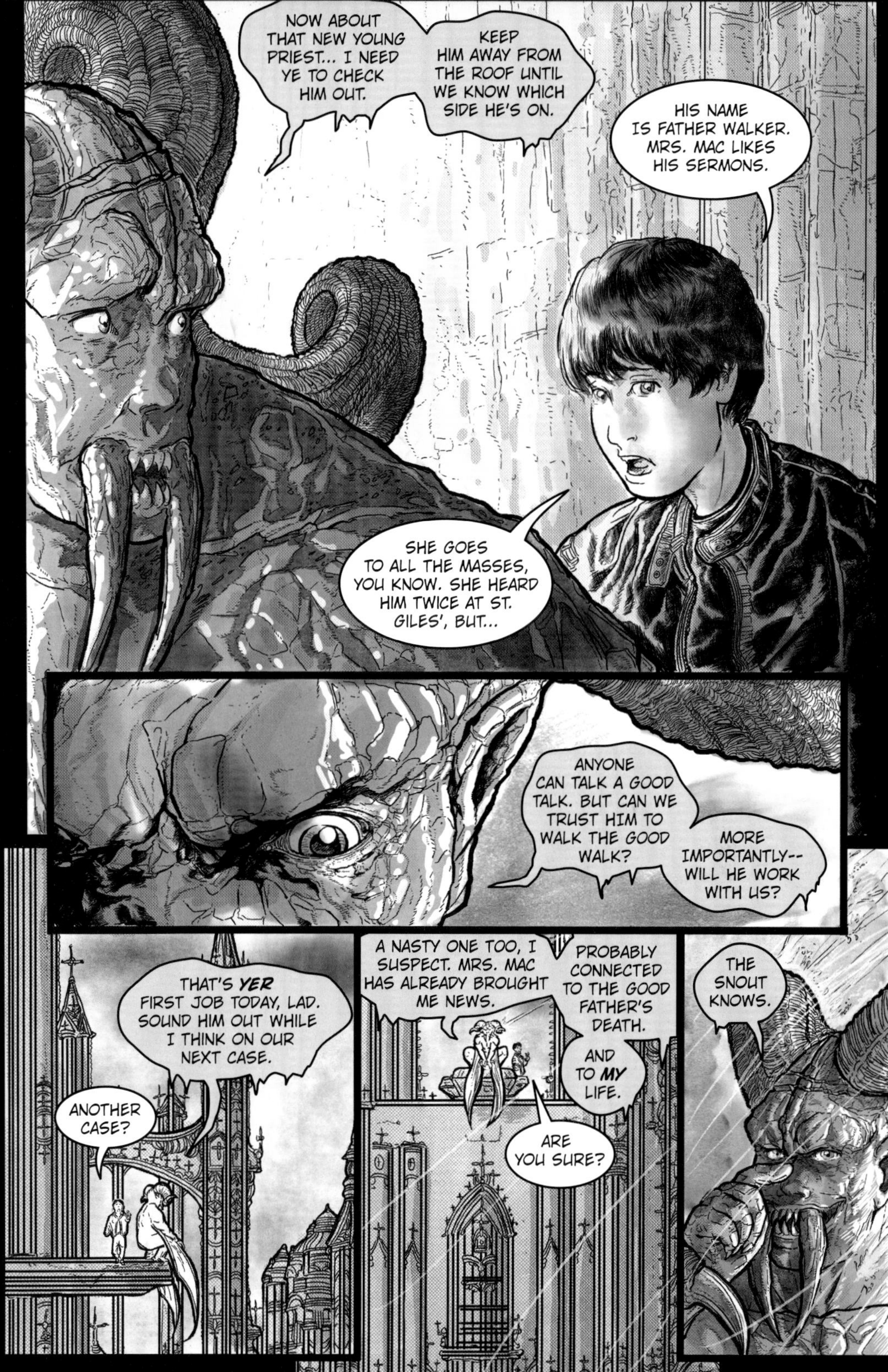
NOW ABOUT THAT NEW YOUNG PRIEST... I NEED YE TO CHECK HIM OUT.
KEEP HIM AWAY FROM THE ROOF UNTIL WE KNOW WHICH SIDE HE'S ON.
HIS NAME IS FATHER WALKER. MRS. MAC LIKES HIS SERMONS.
SHE GOES TO ALL THE MASSES, YOU KNOW. SHE HEARD HIM TWICE AT ST. GILES', BUT...
ANYONE CAN TALK A GOOD TALK. BUT CAN WE TRUST HIM TO WALK THE GOOD WALK?
MORE IMPORTANTLY-- WILL HE WORK WITH US?
THAT'S *YER* FIRST JOB TODAY, LAD. SOUND HIM OUT WHILE I THINK ON OUR NEXT CASE.
ANOTHER CASE?
A NASTY ONE TOO, I SUSPECT. MRS. MAC HAS ALREADY BROUGHT ME NEWS.
PROBABLY CONNECTED TO THE GOOD FATHER'S DEATH.
AND TO *MY* LIFE.
ARE YOU SURE?
THE SNOUT KNOWS.

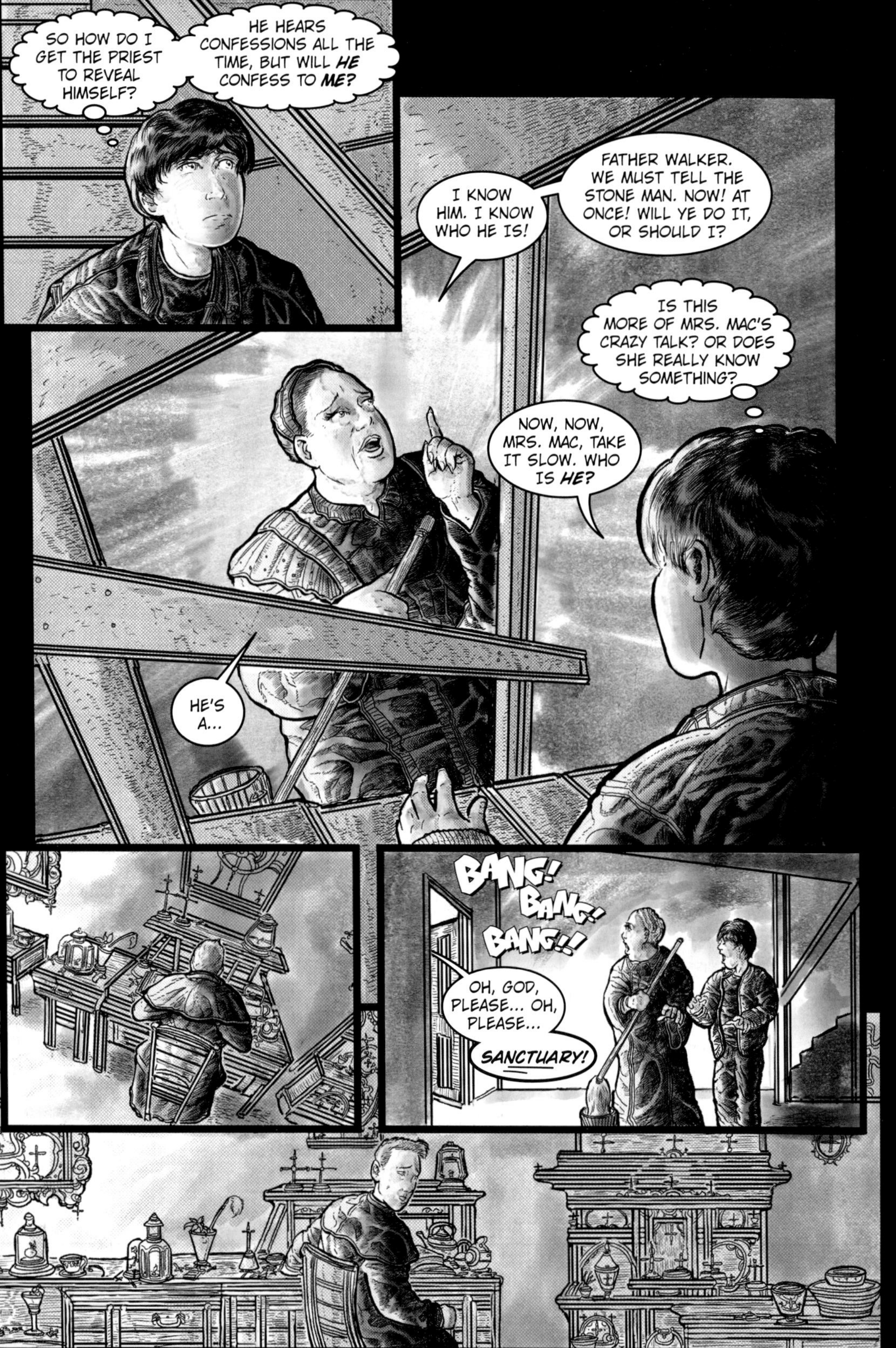
SO HOW DO I GET THE PRIEST TO REVEAL HIMSELF?
HE HEARS CONFESSIONS ALL THE TIME, BUT WILL HE CONFESS TO ME?
I KNOW HIM. I KNOW WHO HE IS!
FATHER WALKER. WE MUST TELL THE STONE MAN. NOW! AT ONCE! WILL YE DO IT, OR SHOULD I?
IS THIS MORE OF MRS. MAC'S CRAZY TALK? OR DOES SHE REALLY KNOW SOMETHING?
NOW, NOW, MRS. MAC, TAKE IT SLOW. WHO IS HE?
HE'S A...
BANG! BANG! BANG!!
OH, GOD, PLEASE... OH, PLEASE... SANCTUARY!

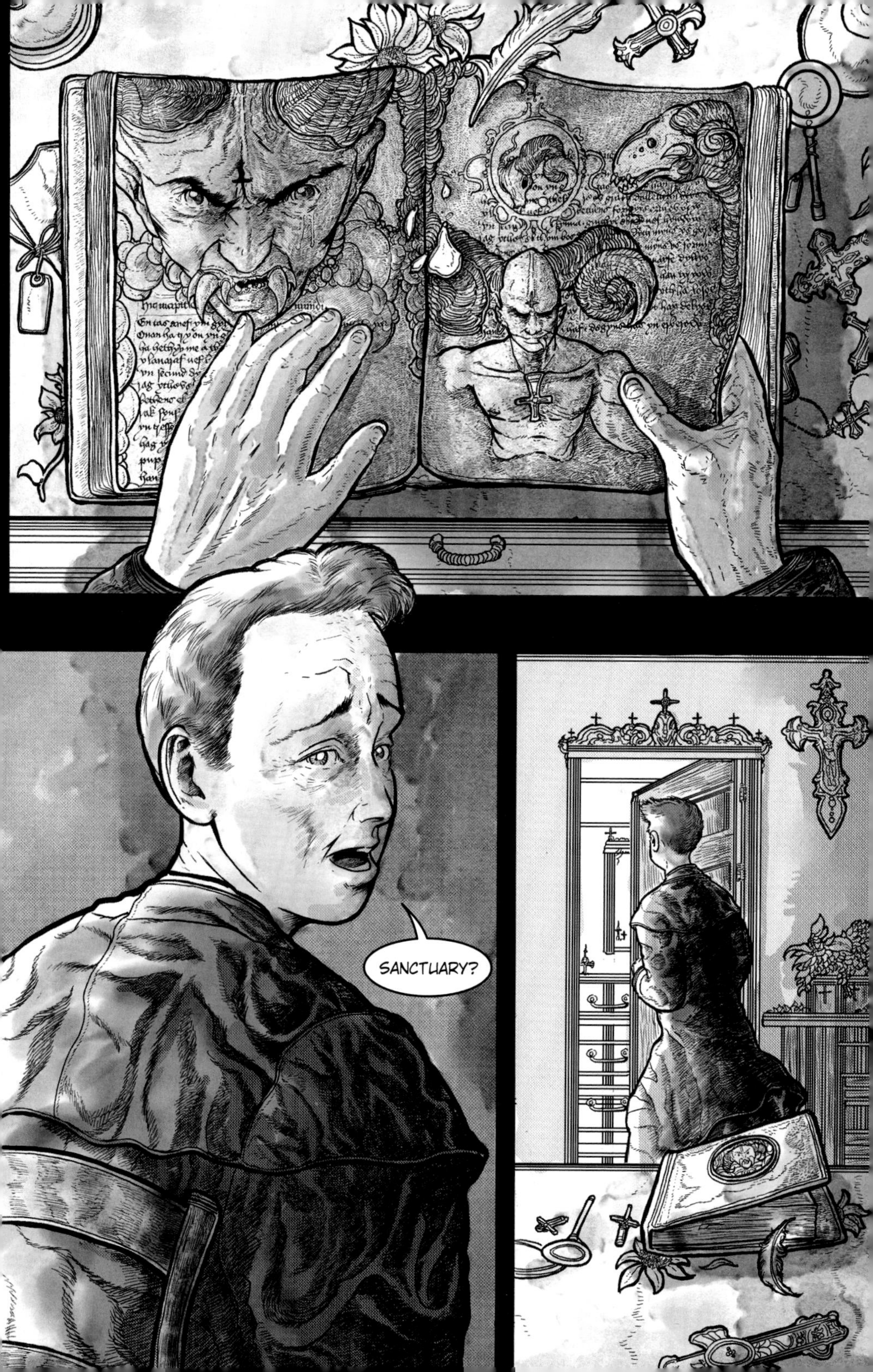
SANCTUARY?

CHAPTER 2
SANCTUARY LAW

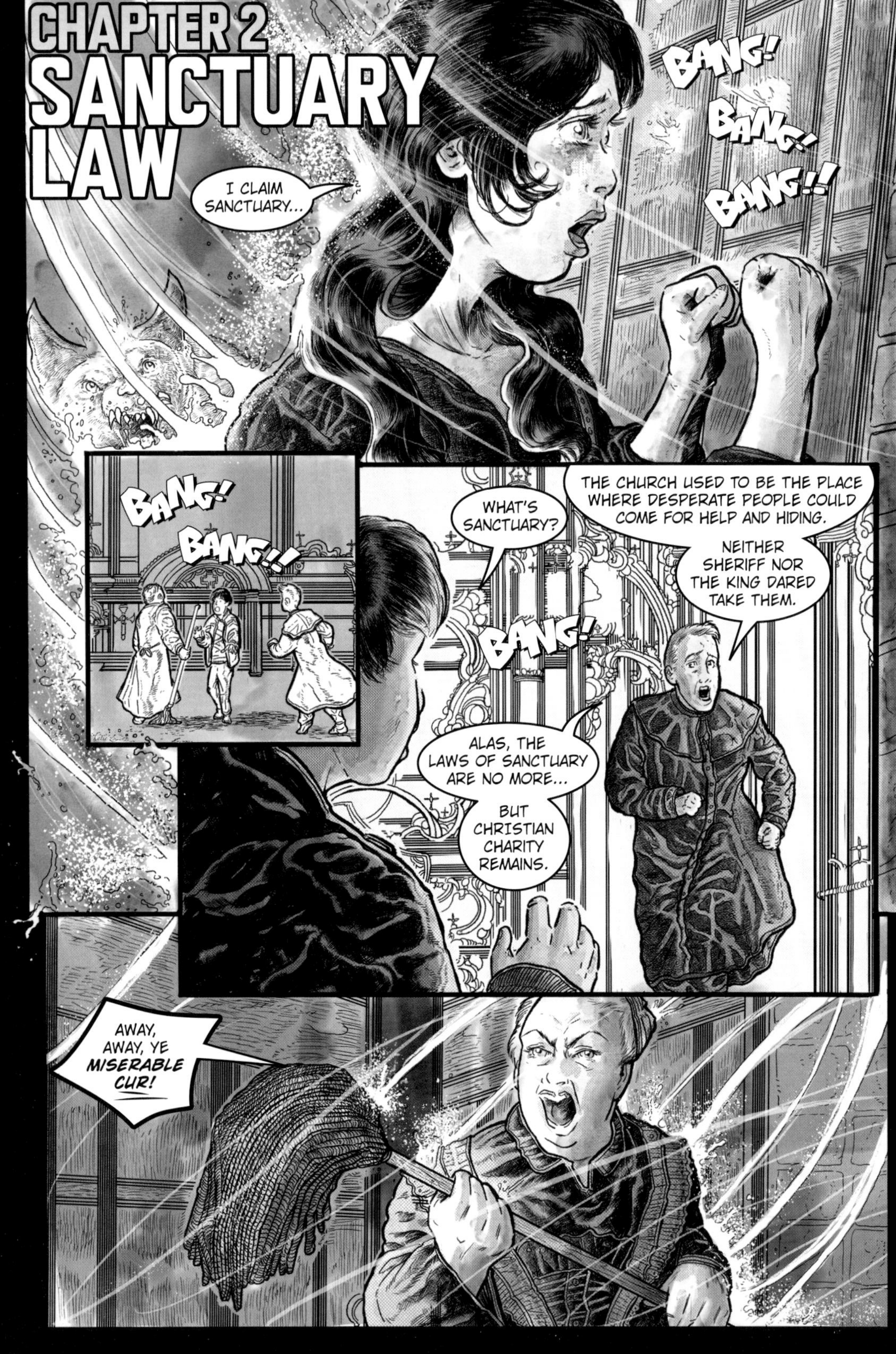

I CLAIM SANCTUARY...
BANG!
BANG!
BANG!!
BANG!
BANG!!
WHAT'S SANCTUARY?
THE CHURCH USED TO BE THE PLACE WHERE DESPERATE PEOPLE COULD COME FOR HELP AND HIDING.
NEITHER SHERIFF NOR THE KING DARED TAKE THEM.
BANG!
ALAS, THE LAWS OF SANCTUARY ARE NO MORE...
BUT CHRISTIAN CHARITY REMAINS.
AWAY, AWAY, YE *MISERABLE CUR!*

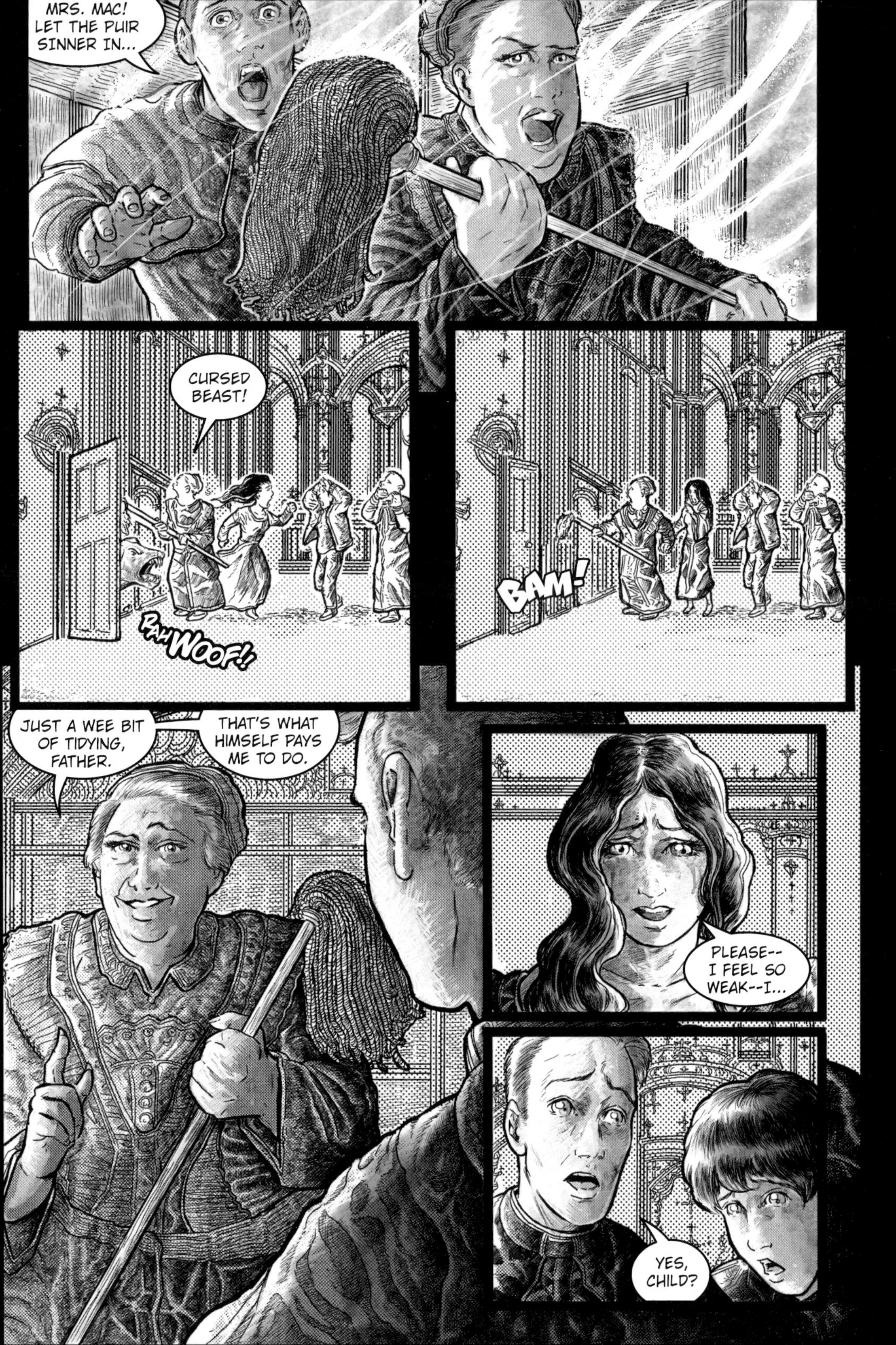

MRS. MAC! LET THE PUIR SINNER IN...
CURSED BEAST!
RAH WOOF!!
BAM!
JUST A WEE BIT OF TIDYING, FATHER.
THAT'S WHAT HIMSELF PAYS ME TO DO.
PLEASE-- I FEEL SO WEAK--I...
YES, CHILD?

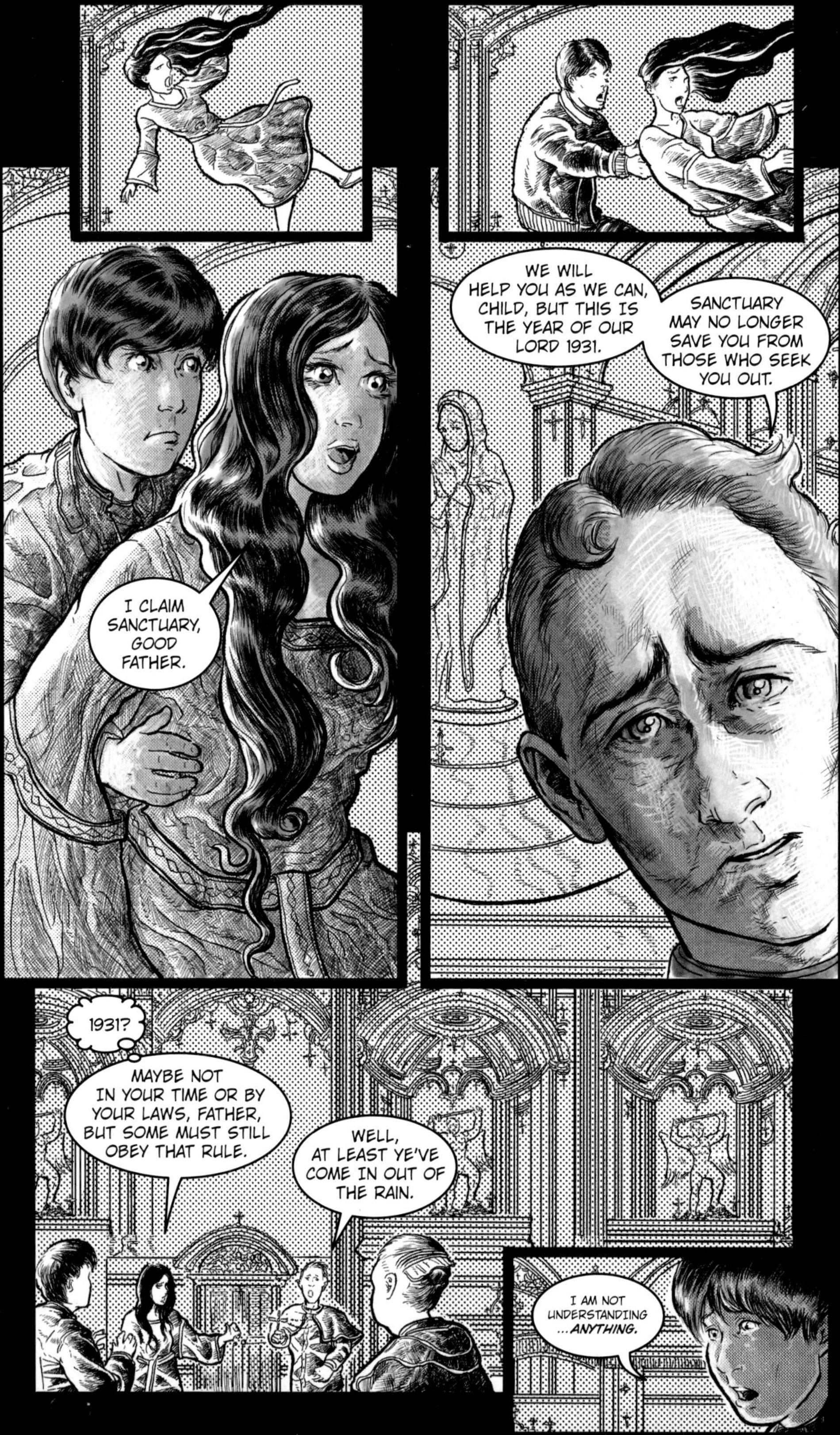
I CLAIM SANCTUARY, GOOD FATHER.
WE WILL HELP YOU AS WE CAN, CHILD, BUT THIS IS THE YEAR OF OUR LORD 1931.
SANCTUARY MAY NO LONGER SAVE YOU FROM THOSE WHO SEEK YOU OUT.
1931?
MAYBE NOT IN YOUR TIME OR BY YOUR LAWS, FATHER, BUT SOME MUST STILL OBEY THAT RULE.
WELL, AT LEAST YE'VE COME IN OUT OF THE RAIN.
I AM NOT UNDERSTANDING ...*ANYTHING.*

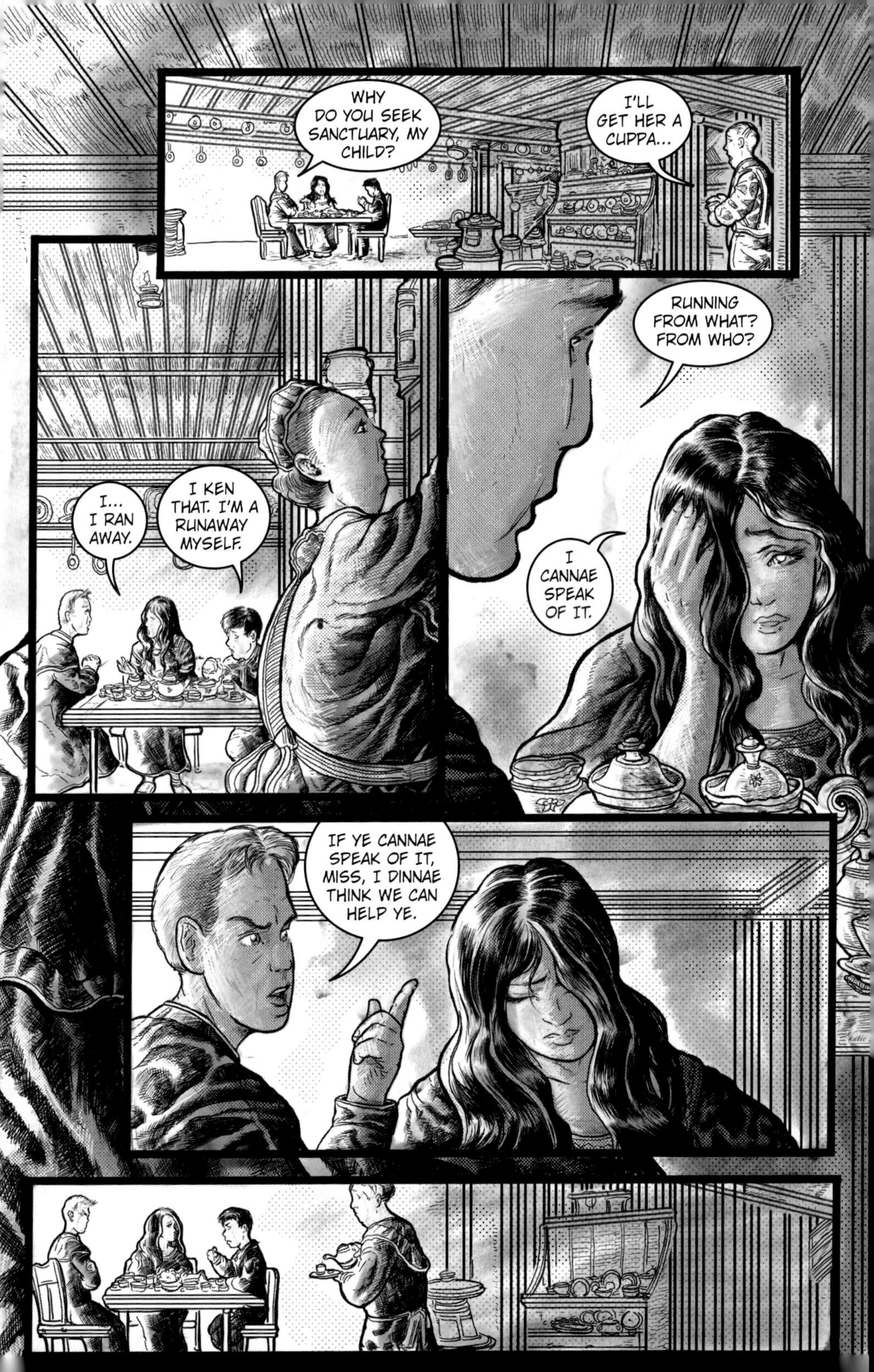
WHY DO YOU SEEK SANCTUARY, MY CHILD?
I'LL GET HER A CUPPA...
I... I RAN AWAY.
I KEN THAT. I'M A RUNAWAY MYSELF.
RUNNING FROM WHAT? FROM WHO?
I CANNAE SPEAK OF IT.
IF YE CANNAE SPEAK OF IT, MISS, I DINNAE THINK WE CAN HELP YE.

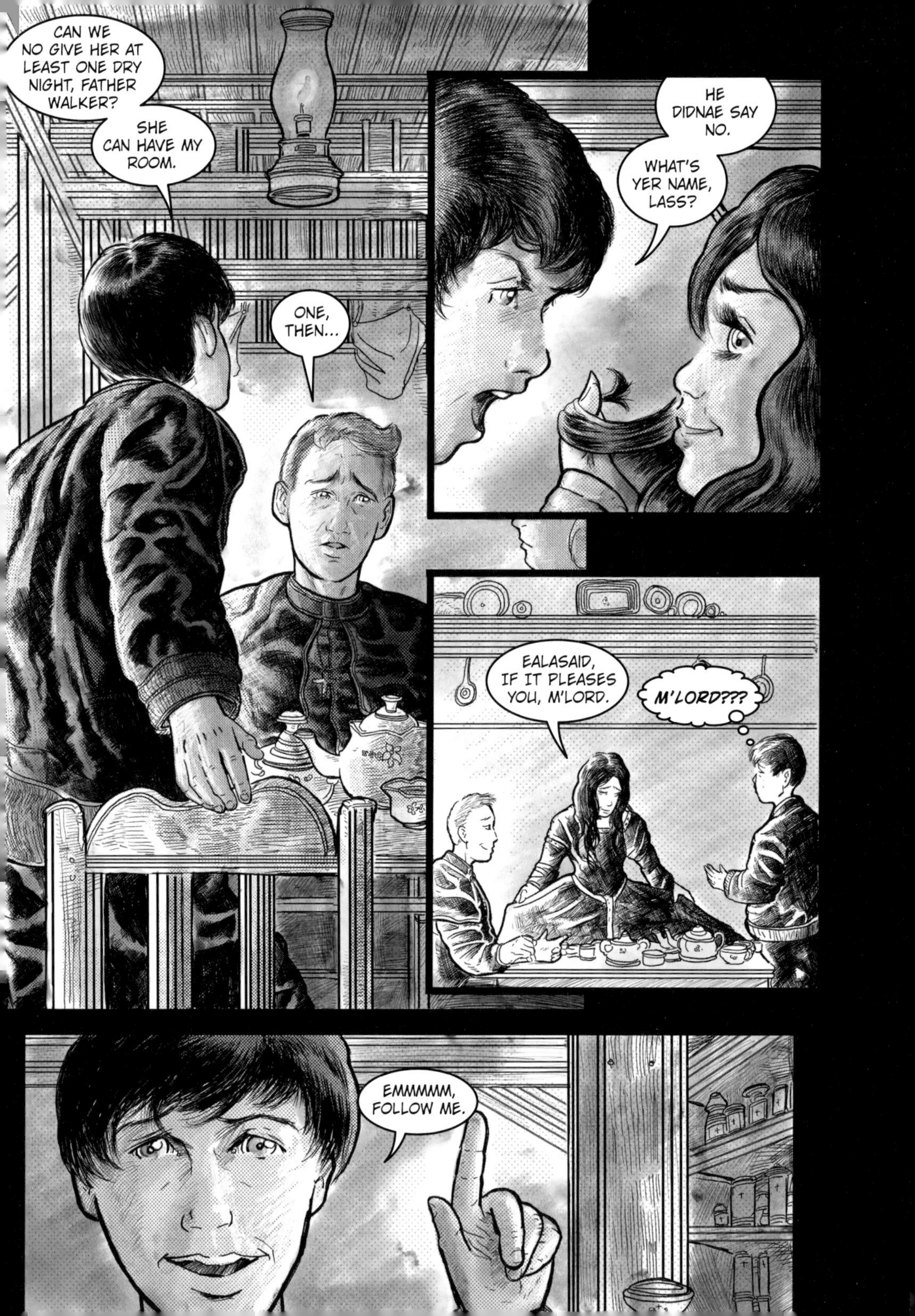
CAN WE NO GIVE HER AT LEAST ONE DRY NIGHT, FATHER WALKER?
SHE CAN HAVE MY ROOM.
ONE, THEN...
HE DIDNAE SAY NO.
WHAT'S YER NAME, LASS?
EALASAID, IF IT PLEASES YOU, M'LORD.
M'LORD???
EMMMMM, FOLLOW ME.

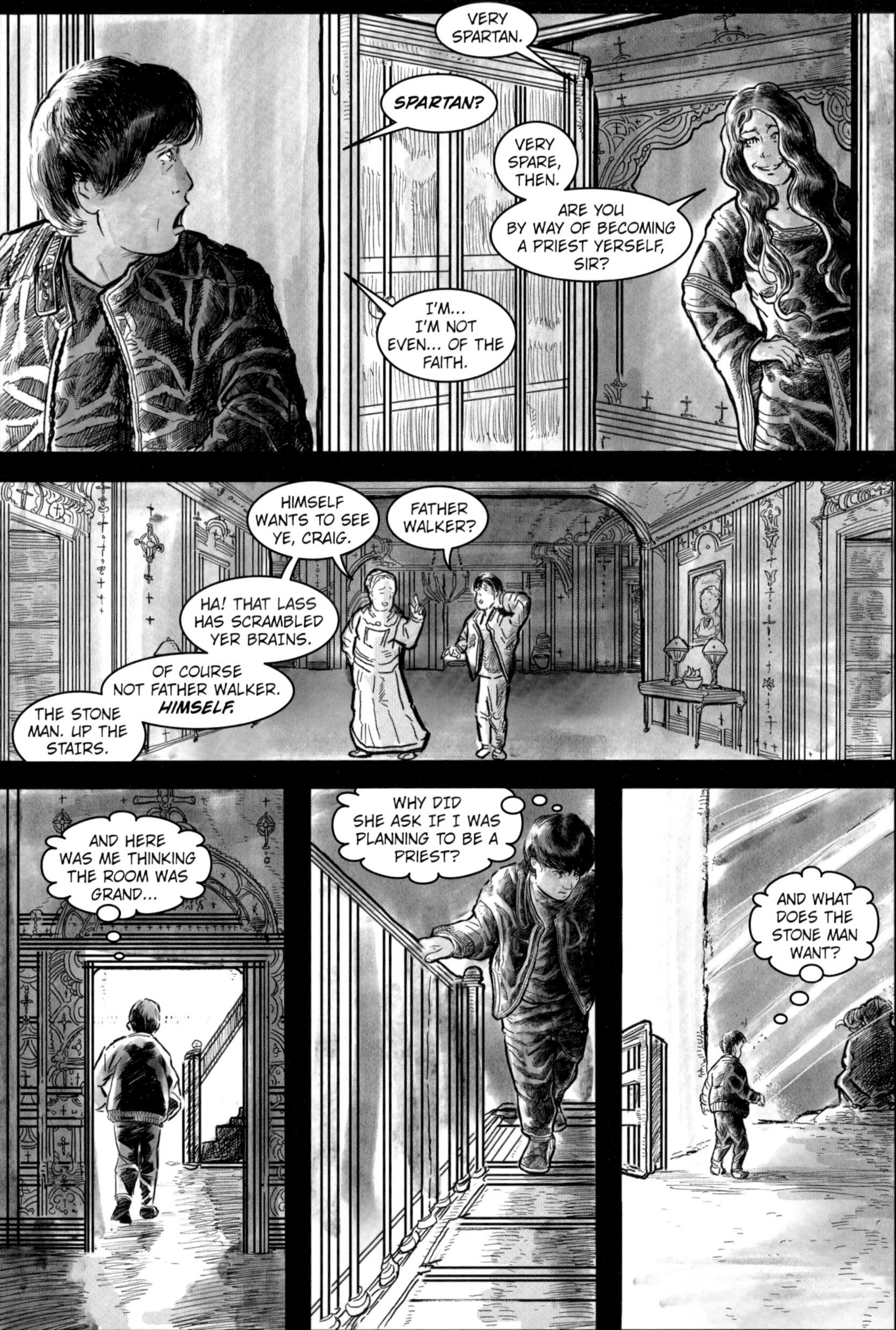
VERY SPARTAN.
SPARTAN?
VERY SPARE, THEN.
ARE YOU BY WAY OF BECOMING A PRIEST YERSELF, SIR?
I'M... I'M NOT EVEN... OF THE FAITH.
HIMSELF WANTS TO SEE YE, CRAIG.
FATHER WALKER?
HA! THAT LASS HAS SCRAMBLED YER BRAINS.
OF COURSE NOT FATHER WALKER. HIMSELF.
THE STONE MAN. UP THE STAIRS.
AND HERE WAS ME THINKING THE ROOM WAS GRAND...
WHY DID SHE ASK IF I WAS PLANNING TO BE A PRIEST?
AND WHAT DOES THE STONE MAN WANT?

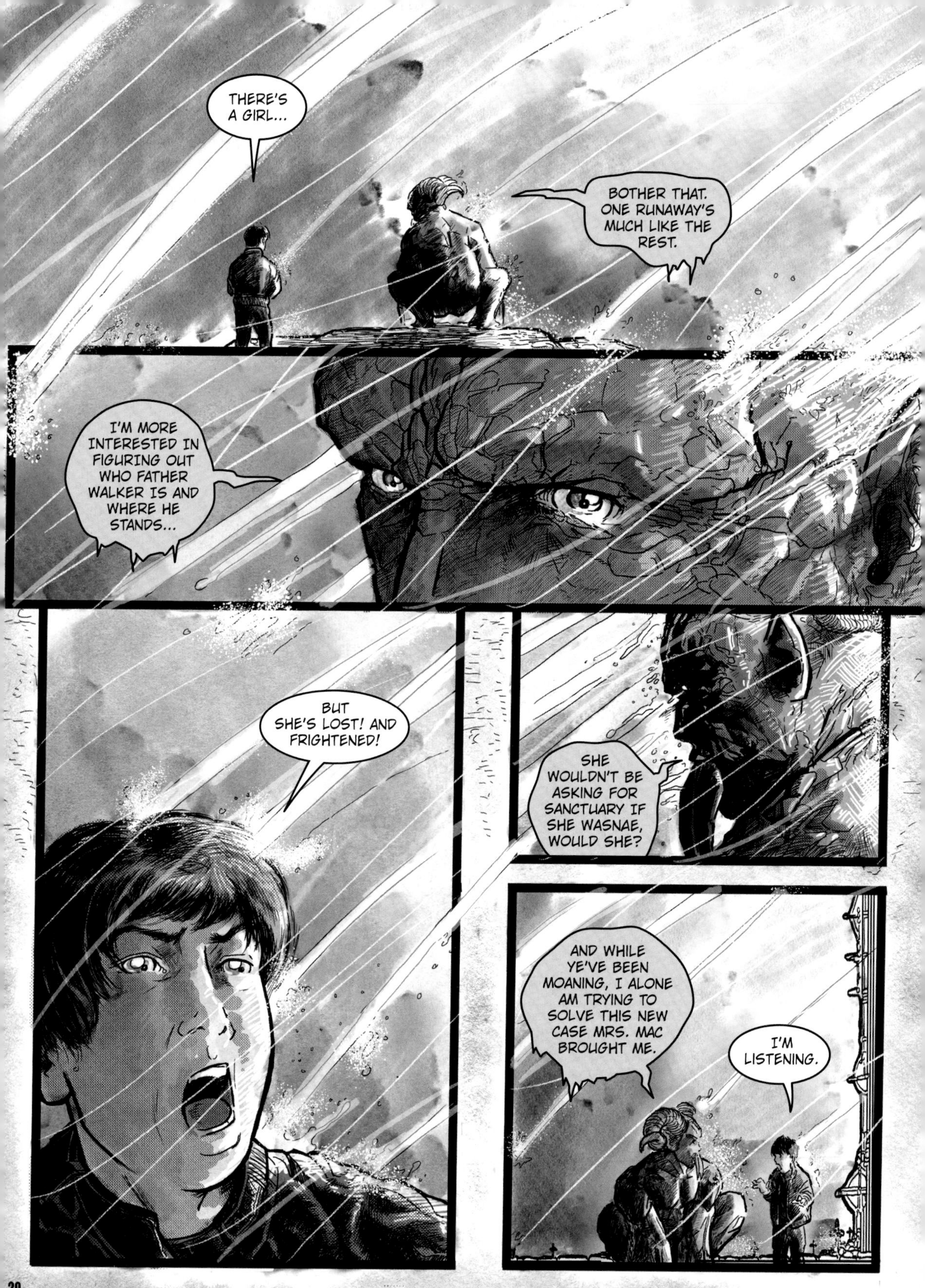
THERE'S A GIRL...
BOTHER THAT. ONE RUNAWAY'S MUCH LIKE THE REST.
I'M MORE INTERESTED IN FIGURING OUT WHO FATHER WALKER IS AND WHERE HE STANDS...
BUT SHE'S LOST! AND FRIGHTENED!
SHE WOULDN'T BE ASKING FOR SANCTUARY IF SHE WASNAE, WOULD SHE?
AND WHILE YE'VE BEEN MOANING, I ALONE AM TRYING TO SOLVE THIS NEW CASE MRS. MAC BROUGHT ME.
I'M LISTENING.

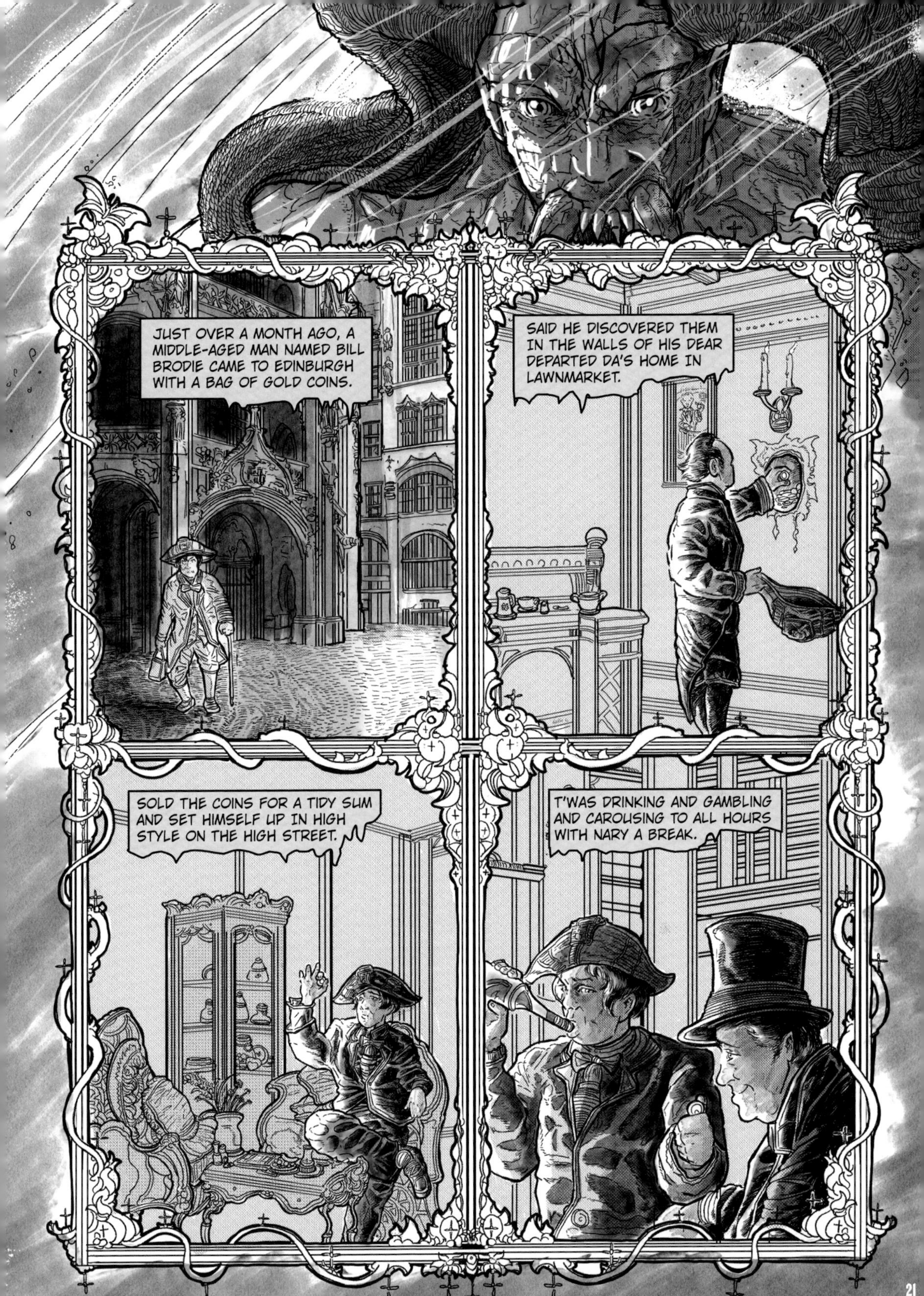
JUST OVER A MONTH AGO, A MIDDLE-AGED MAN NAMED BILL BRODIE CAME TO EDINBURGH WITH A BAG OF GOLD COINS.
SAID HE DISCOVERED THEM IN THE WALLS OF HIS DEAR DEPARTED DA'S HOME IN LAWNMARKET.
SOLD THE COINS FOR A TIDY SUM AND SET HIMSELF UP IN HIGH STYLE ON THE HIGH STREET.
T'WAS DRINKING AND GAMBLING AND CAROUSING TO ALL HOURS WITH NARY A BREAK.

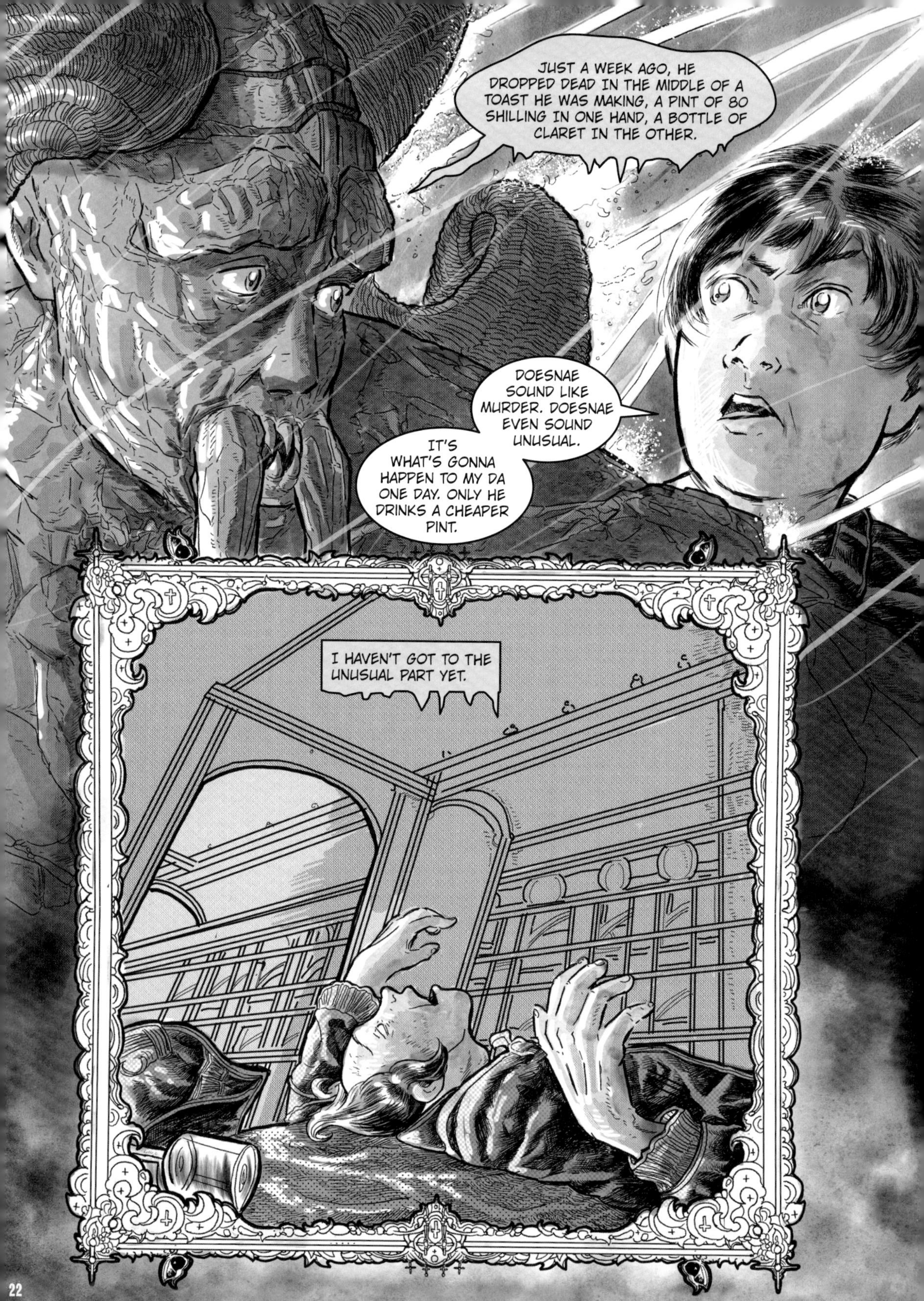
JUST A WEEK AGO, HE DROPPED DEAD IN THE MIDDLE OF A TOAST HE WAS MAKING, A PINT OF 80 SHILLING IN ONE HAND, A BOTTLE OF CLARET IN THE OTHER.
DOESNAE SOUND LIKE MURDER. DOESNAE EVEN SOUND UNUSUAL.
IT'S WHAT'S GONNA HAPPEN TO MY DA ONE DAY. ONLY HE DRINKS A CHEAPER PINT.
I HAVEN'T GOT TO THE UNUSUAL PART YET.

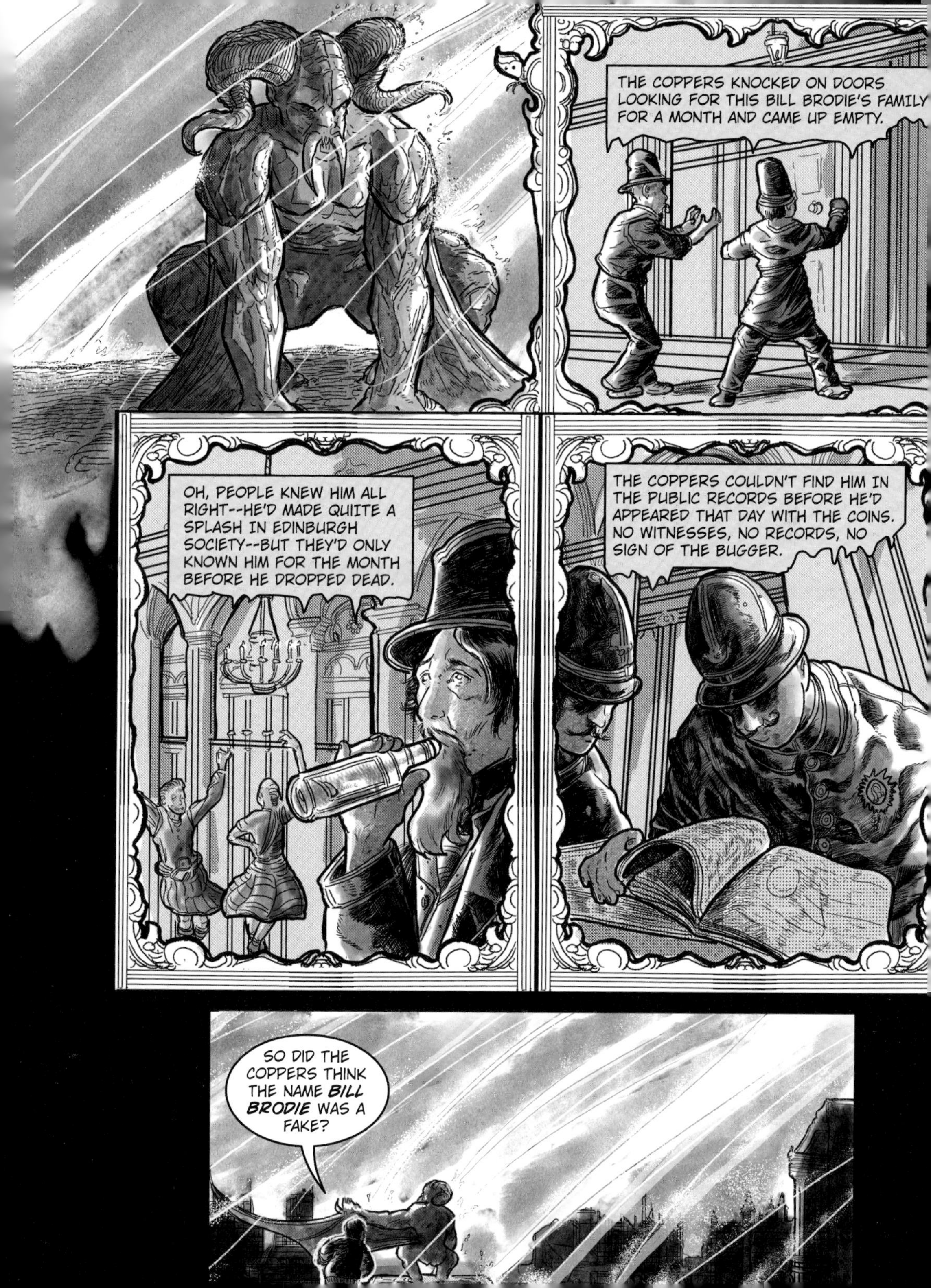
THE COPPERS KNOCKED ON DOORS LOOKING FOR THIS BILL BRODIE'S FAMILY FOR A MONTH AND CAME UP EMPTY.
OH, PEOPLE KNEW HIM ALL RIGHT--HE'D MADE QUIITE A SPLASH IN EDINBURGH SOCIETY--BUT THEY'D ONLY KNOWN HIM FOR THE MONTH BEFORE HE DROPPED DEAD.
THE COPPERS COULDN'T FIND HIM IN THE PUBLIC RECORDS BEFORE HE'D APPEARED THAT DAY WITH THE COINS. NO WITNESSES, NO RECORDS, NO SIGN OF THE BUGGER.
SO DID THE COPPERS THINK THE NAME ***BILL BRODIE*** WAS A FAKE?

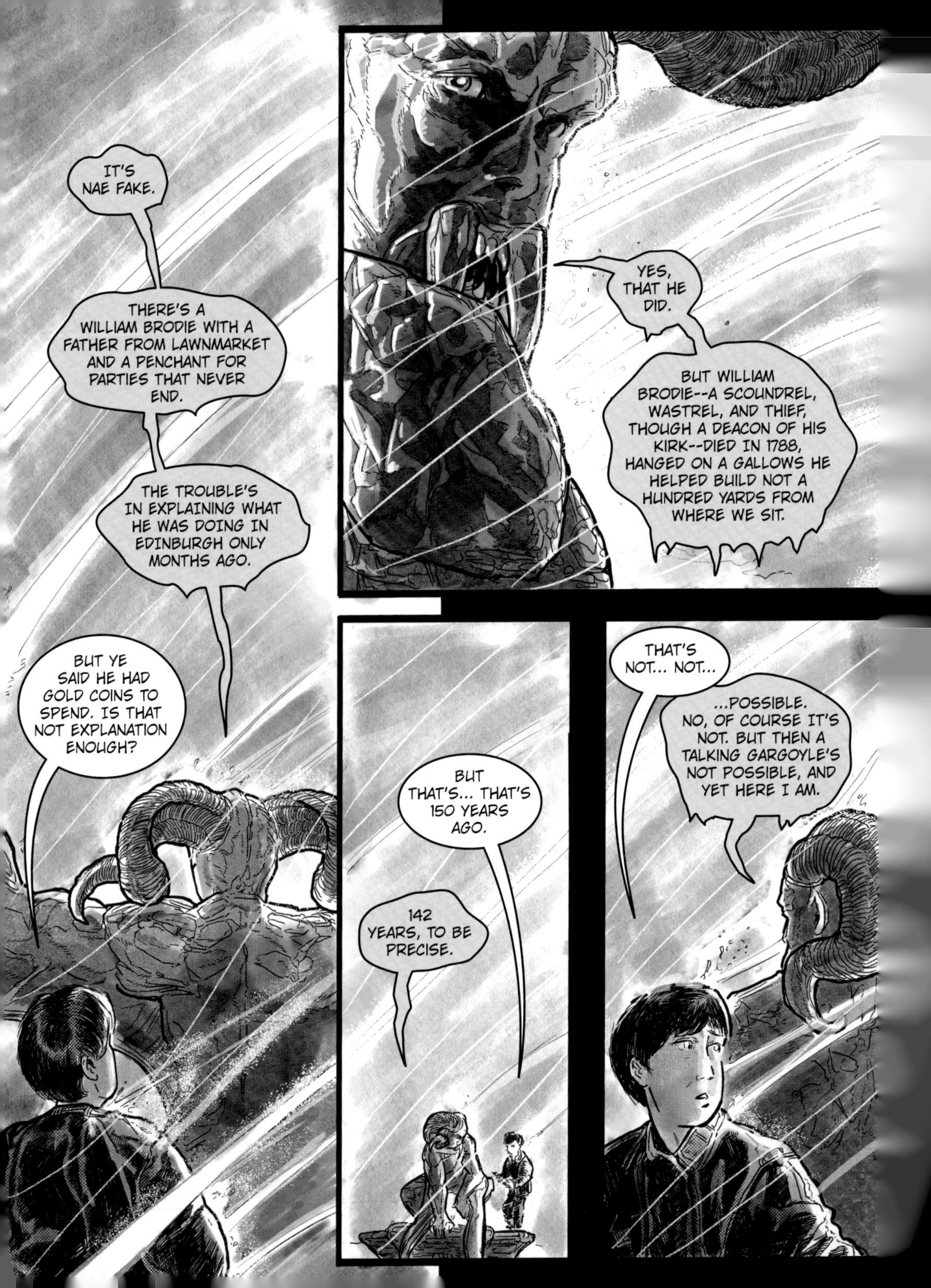
IT'S NAE FAKE.
THERE'S A WILLIAM BRODIE WITH A FATHER FROM LAWNMARKET AND A PENCHANT FOR PARTIES THAT NEVER END.
THE TROUBLE'S IN EXPLAINING WHAT HE WAS DOING IN EDINBURGH ONLY MONTHS AGO.
YES, THAT HE DID.
BUT WILLIAM BRODIE--A SCOUNDREL, WASTREL, AND THIEF, THOUGH A DEACON OF HIS KIRK--DIED IN 1788, HANGED ON A GALLOWS HE HELPED BUILD NOT A HUNDRED YARDS FROM WHERE WE SIT.
BUT YE SAID HE HAD GOLD COINS TO SPEND. IS THAT NOT EXPLANATION ENOUGH?
BUT THAT'S... THAT'S 150 YEARS AGO.
142 YEARS, TO BE PRECISE.
THAT'S NOT... NOT...
...POSSIBLE. NO, OF COURSE IT'S NOT. BUT THEN A TALKING GARGOYLE'S NOT POSSIBLE, AND YET HERE I AM.

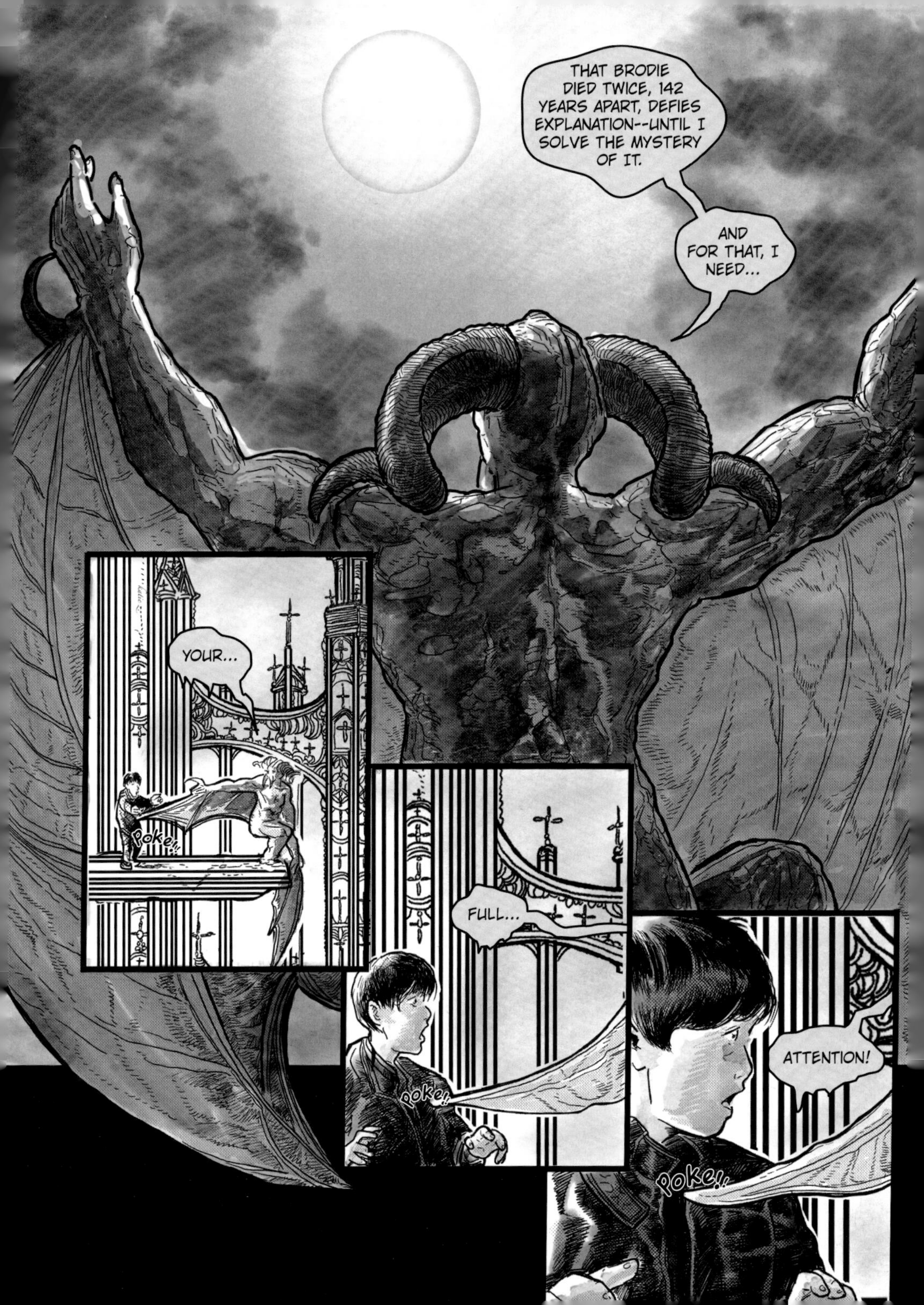
THAT BRODIE DIED TWICE, 142 YEARS APART, DEFIES EXPLANATION--UNTIL I SOLVE THE MYSTERY OF IT.
AND FOR THAT, I NEED...
YOUR...
POKE!!
FULL...
POKE!!
ATTENTION!
POKE!!

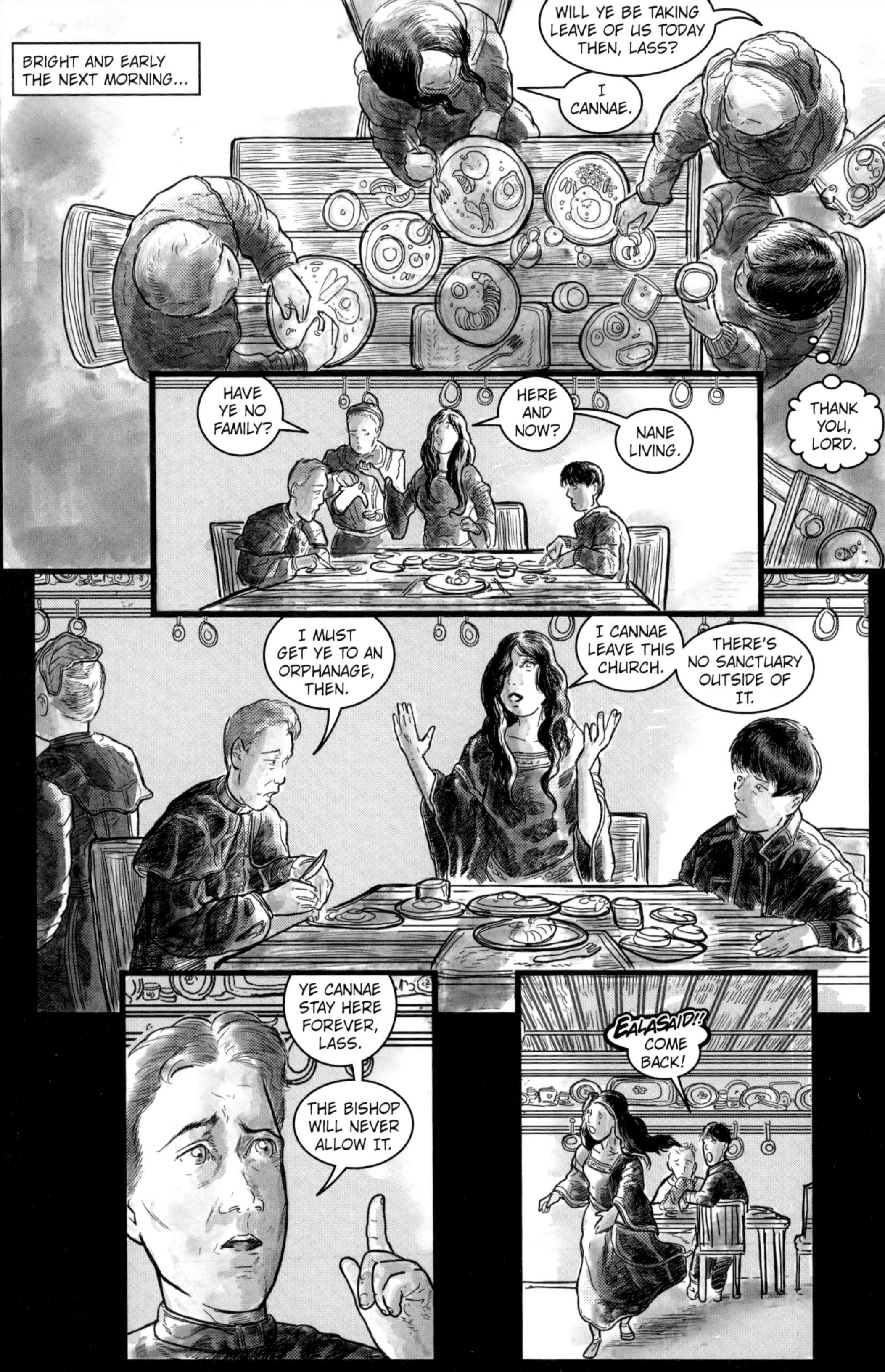
BRIGHT AND EARLY THE NEXT MORNING...
WILL YE BE TAKING LEAVE OF US TODAY THEN, LASS?
I CANNAE.
THANK YOU, LORD.
HAVE YE NO FAMILY?
HERE AND NOW?
NANE LIVING.
I MUST GET YE TO AN ORPHANAGE, THEN.
I CANNAE LEAVE THIS CHURCH.
THERE'S NO SANCTUARY OUTSIDE OF IT.
YE CANNAE STAY HERE FOREVER, LASS.
THE BISHOP WILL NEVER ALLOW IT.
EALASAID!! COME BACK!

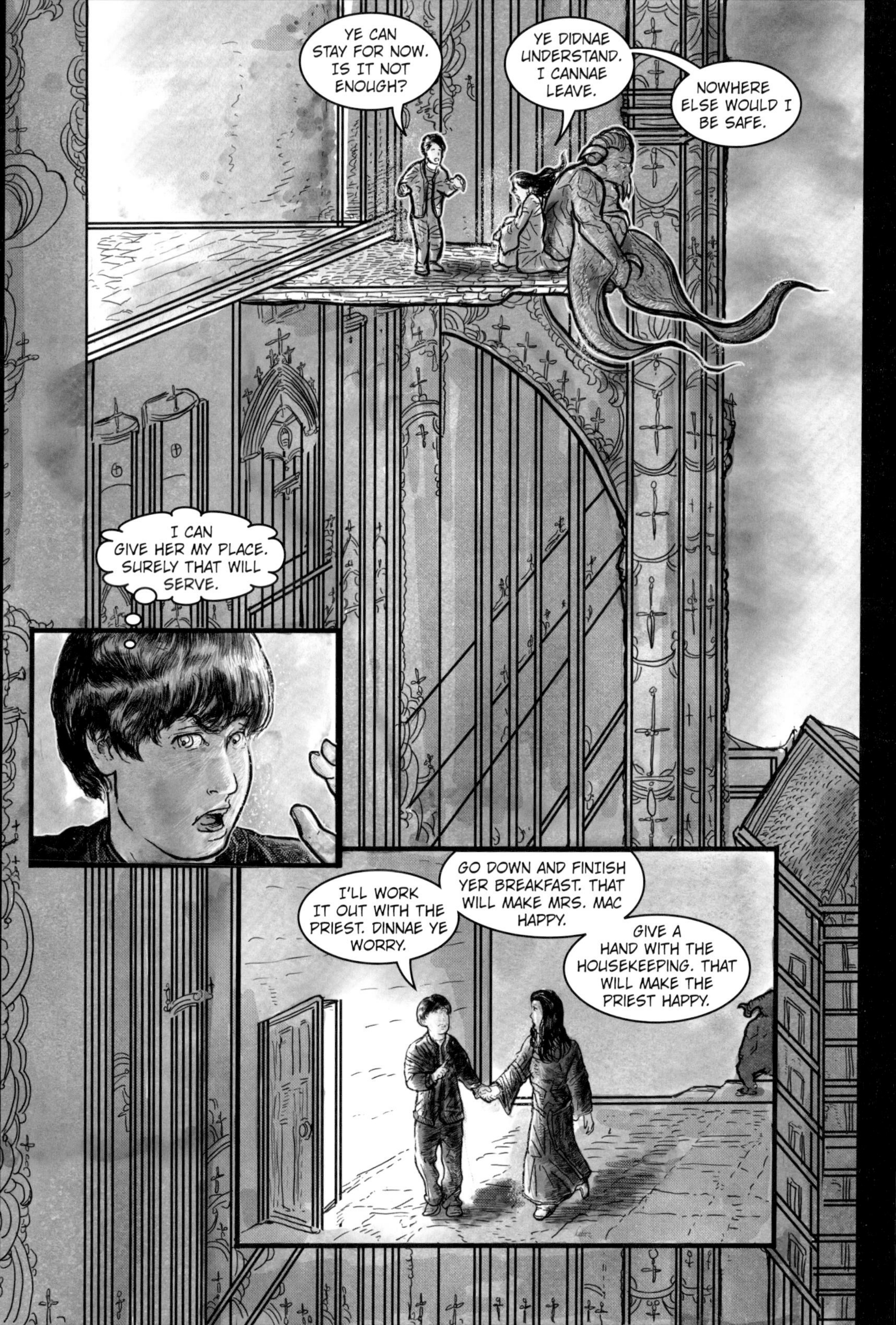
YE CAN STAY FOR NOW. IS IT NOT ENOUGH?
YE DIDNAE UNDERSTAND. I CANNAE LEAVE.
NOWHERE ELSE WOULD I BE SAFE.
I CAN GIVE HER MY PLACE. SURELY THAT WILL SERVE.
I'LL WORK IT OUT WITH THE PRIEST. DINNAE YE WORRY.
GO DOWN AND FINIISH YER BREAKFAST. THAT WILL MAKE MRS. MAC HAPPY.
GIVE A HAND WITH THE HOUSEKEEPING. THAT WILL MAKE THE PRIEST HAPPY.

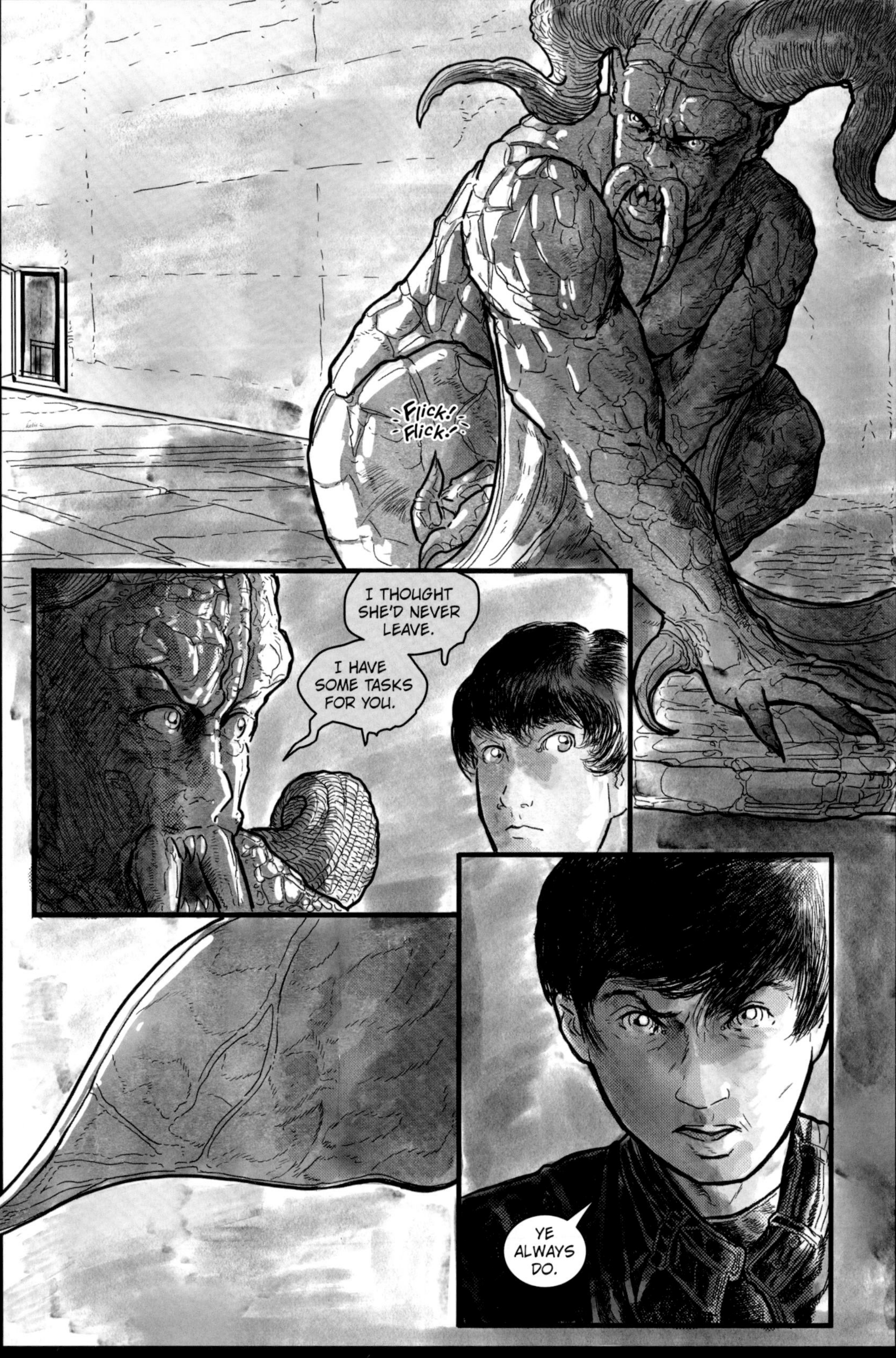

Flick! Flick!
I THOUGHT SHE'D NEVER LEAVE.
I HAVE SOME TASKS FOR YOU.
YE ALWAYS DO.

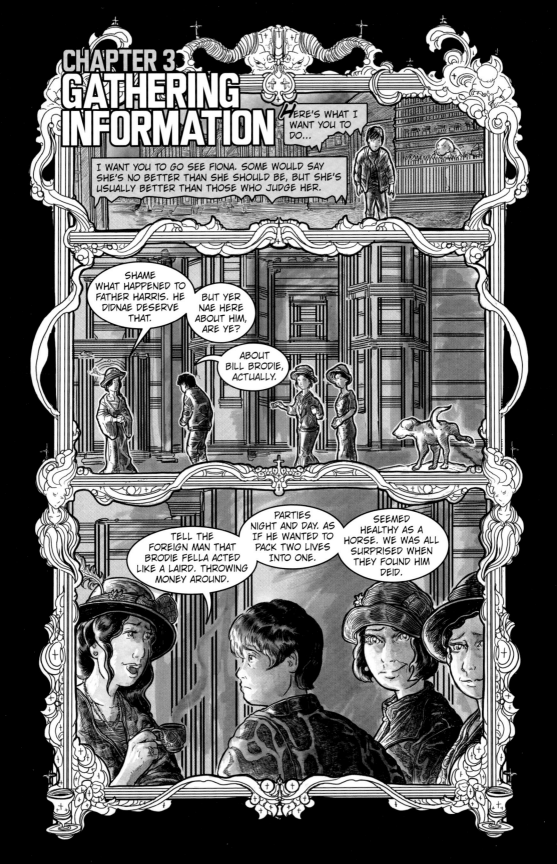

CHAPTER 3
GATHERING INFORMATION

HERE'S WHAT I WANT YOU TO DO...

I WANT YOU TO GO SEE FIONA. SOME WOULD SAY SHE'S NO BETTER THAN SHE SHOULD BE, BUT SHE'S USUALLY BETTER THAN THOSE WHO JUDGE HER.

SHAME WHAT HAPPENED TO FATHER HARRIS. HE DIDNAE DESERVE THAT.

BUT YER NAE HERE ABOUT HIM, ARE YE?

ABOUT BILL BRODIE, ACTUALLY.

TELL THE FOREIGN MAN THAT BRODIE FELLA ACTED LIKE A LAIRD. THROWING MONEY AROUND.

PARTIES NIGHT AND DAY. AS IF HE WANTED TO PACK TWO LIVES INTO ONE.

SEEMED HEALTHY AS A HORSE. WE WAS ALL SURPRISED WHEN THEY FOUND HIM DEID.

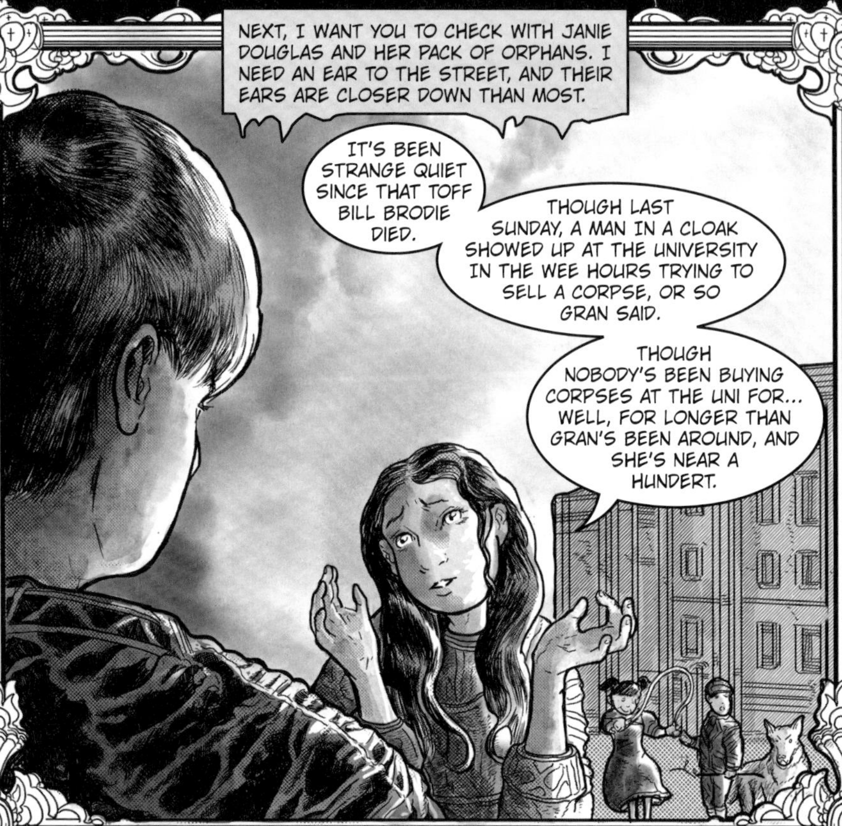
NEXT, I WANT YOU TO CHECK WITH JANIE DOUGLAS AND HER PACK OF ORPHANS. I NEED AN EAR TO THE STREET, AND THEIR EARS ARE CLOSER DOWN THAN MOST.
IT'S BEEN STRANGE QUIET SINCE THAT TOFF BILL BRODIE DIED.
THOUGH LAST SUNDAY, A MAN IN A CLOAK SHOWED UP AT THE UNIVERSITY IN THE WEE HOURS TRYING TO SELL A CORPSE, OR SO GRAN SAID.
THOUGH NOBODY'S BEEN BUYING CORPSES AT THE UNI FOR... WELL, FOR LONGER THAN GRAN'S BEEN AROUND, AND SHE'S NEAR A HUNDERT.

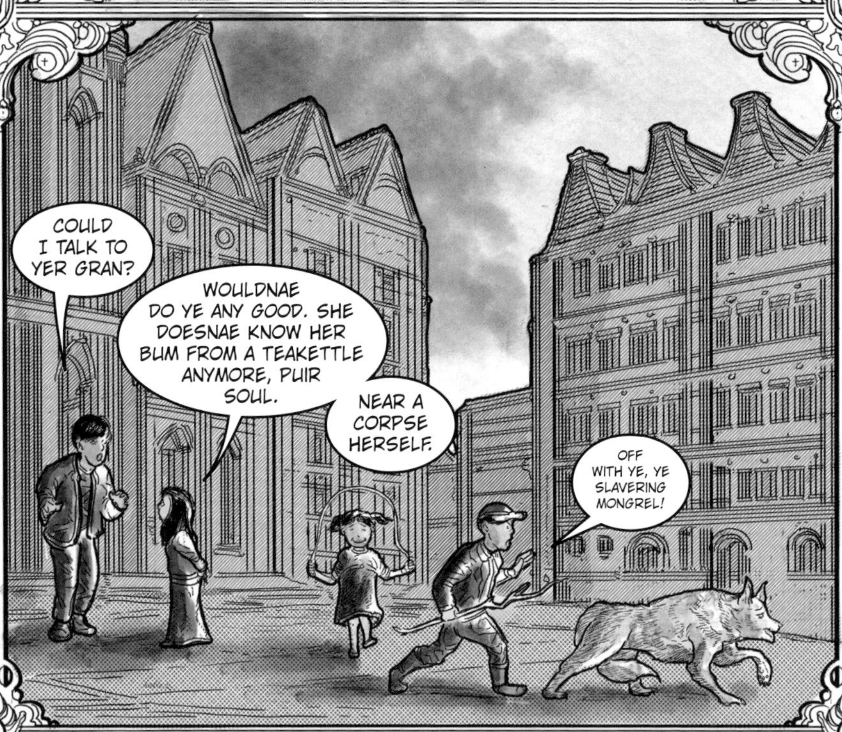
COULD I TALK TO YER GRAN?
WOULDNAE DO YE ANY GOOD. SHE DOESNAE KNOW HER BUM FROM A TEAKETTLE ANYMORE, PUIR SOUL.
NEAR A CORPSE HERSELF.
OFF WITH YE, YE SLAVERING MONGREL!

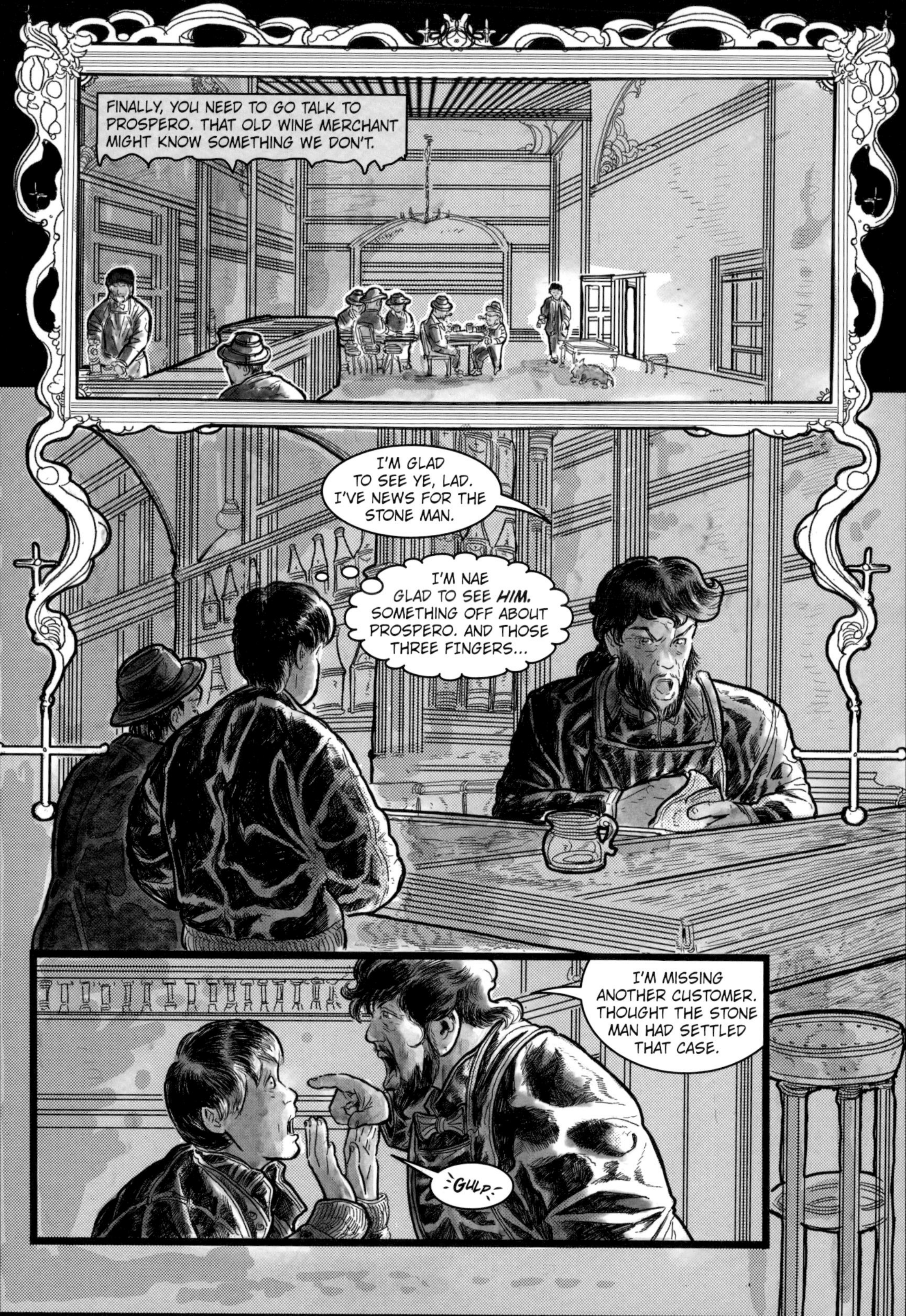
FINALLY, YOU NEED TO GO TALK TO PROSPERO. THAT OLD WINE MERCHANT MIGHT KNOW SOMETHING WE DON'T.
I'M GLAD TO SEE YE, LAD. I'VE NEWS FOR THE STONE MAN.
I'M NAE GLAD TO SEE HIM. SOMETHING OFF ABOUT PROSPERO. AND THOSE THREE FINGERS...
I'M MISSING ANOTHER CUSTOMER. THOUGHT THE STONE MAN HAD SETTLED THAT CASE.
GULP

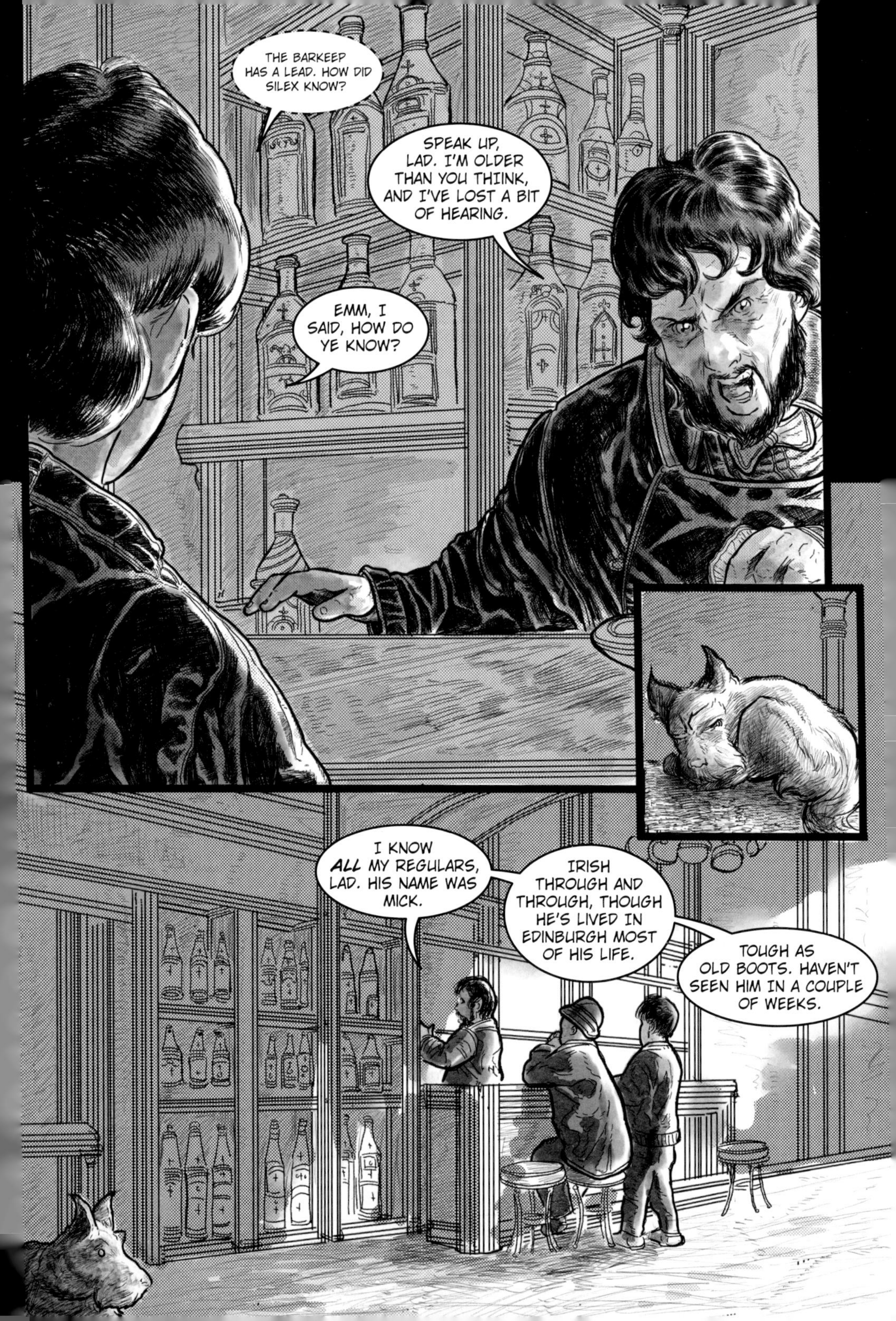
THE BARKEEP HAS A LEAD. HOW DID SILEX KNOW?
SPEAK UP, LAD. I'M OLDER THAN YOU THINK, AND I'VE LOST A BIT OF HEARING.
EMM, I SAID, HOW DO YE KNOW?
I KNOW ALL MY REGULARS, LAD. HIS NAME WAS MICK.
IRISH THROUGH AND THROUGH, THOUGH HE'S LIVED IN EDINBURGH MOST OF HIS LIFE.
TOUGH AS OLD BOOTS. HAVEN'T SEEN HIM IN A COUPLE OF WEEKS.

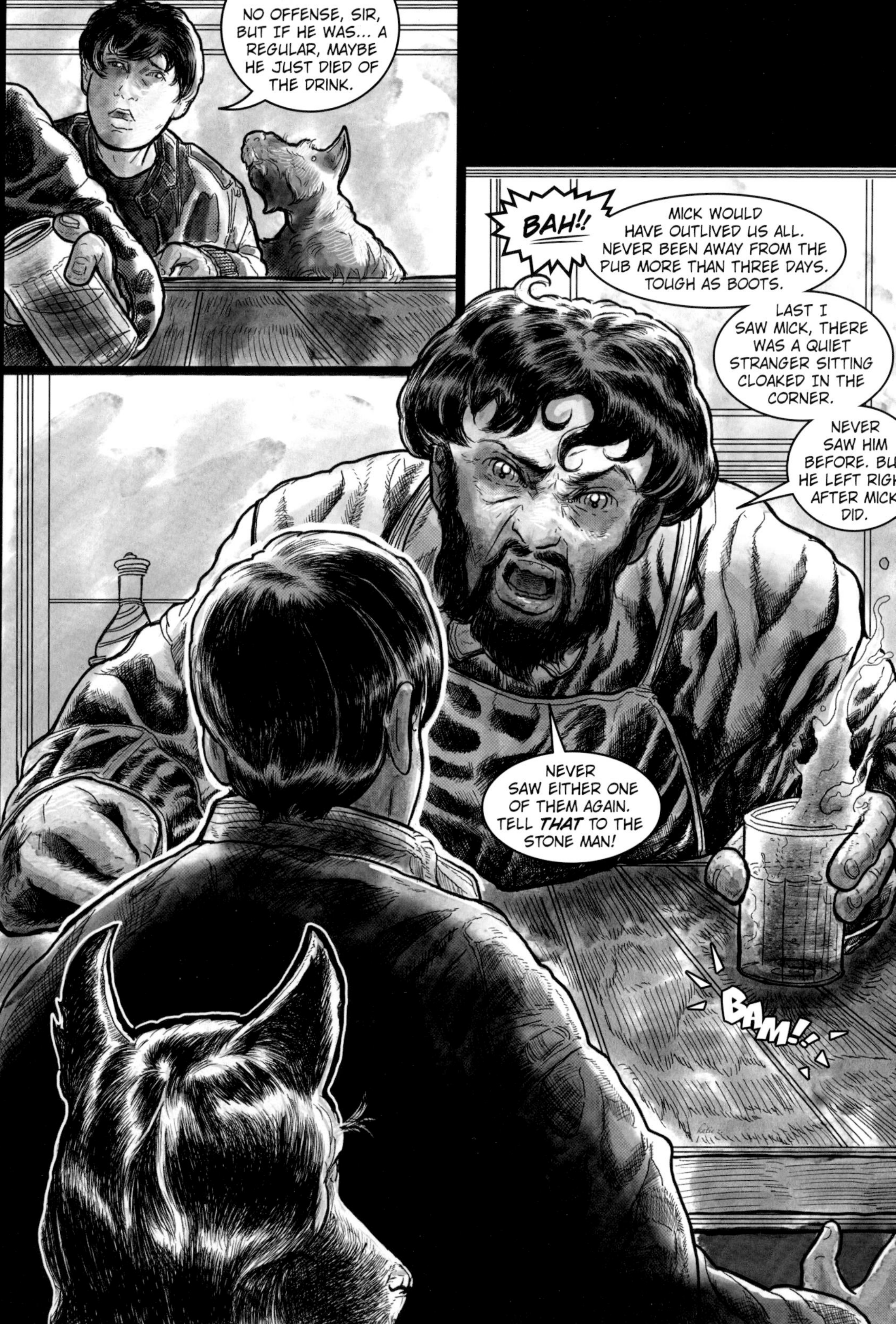
NO OFFENSE, SIR, BUT IF HE WAS... A REGULAR, MAYBE HE JUST DIED OF THE DRINK.
BAH!!
MICK WOULD HAVE OUTLIVED US ALL. NEVER BEEN AWAY FROM THE PUB MORE THAN THREE DAYS. TOUGH AS BOOTS.
LAST I SAW MICK, THERE WAS A QUIET STRANGER SITTING CLOAKED IN THE CORNER.
NEVER SAW HIM BEFORE. BU HE LEFT RIGH AFTER MICK DID.
NEVER SAW EITHER ONE OF THEM AGAIN. TELL *THAT* TO THE STONE MAN!
BAM!!

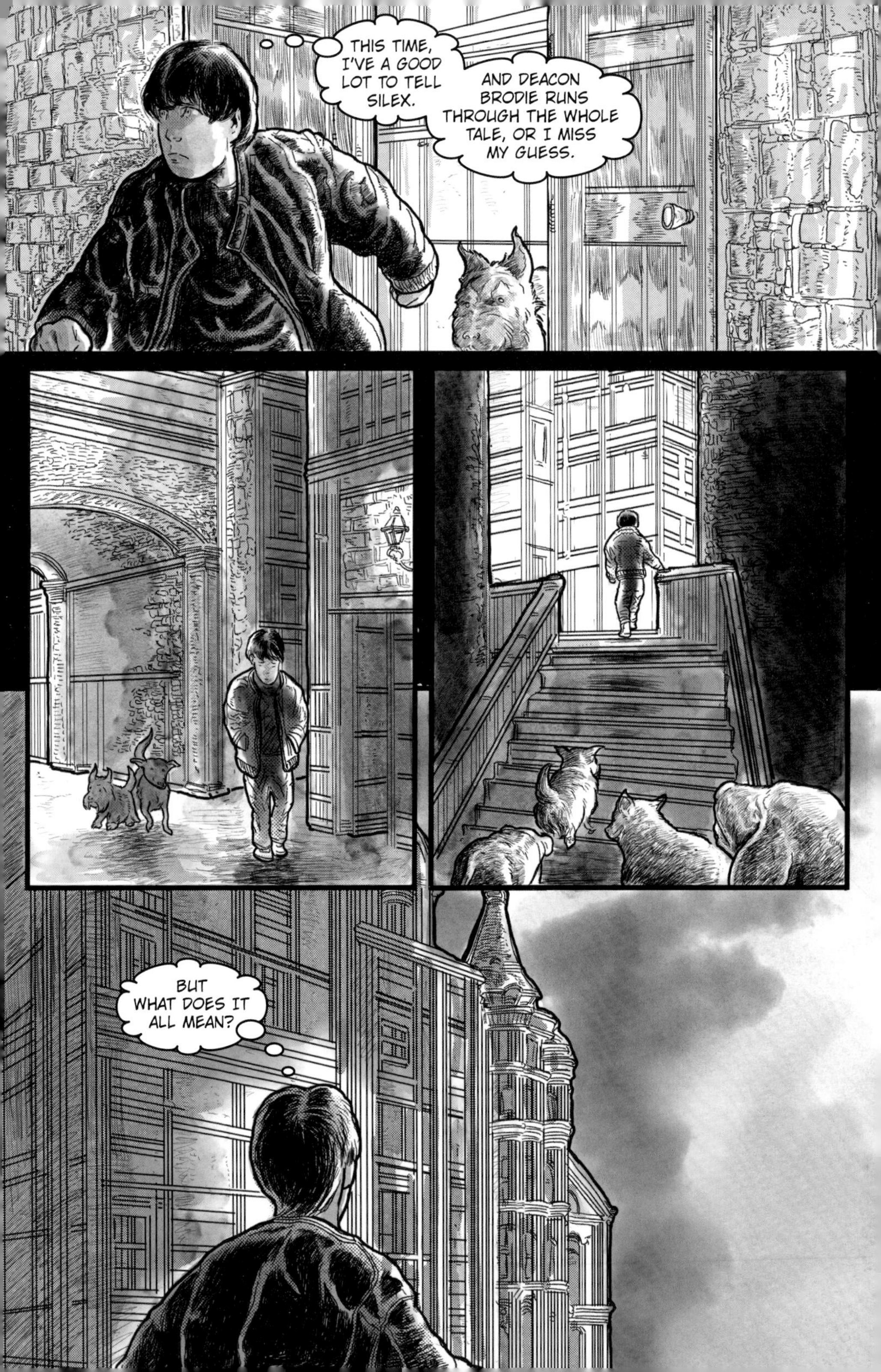
THIS TIME, I'VE A GOOD LOT TO TELL SILEX.
AND DEACON BRODIE RUNS THROUGH THE WHOLE TALE, OR I MISS MY GUESS.
BUT WHAT DOES IT ALL MEAN?

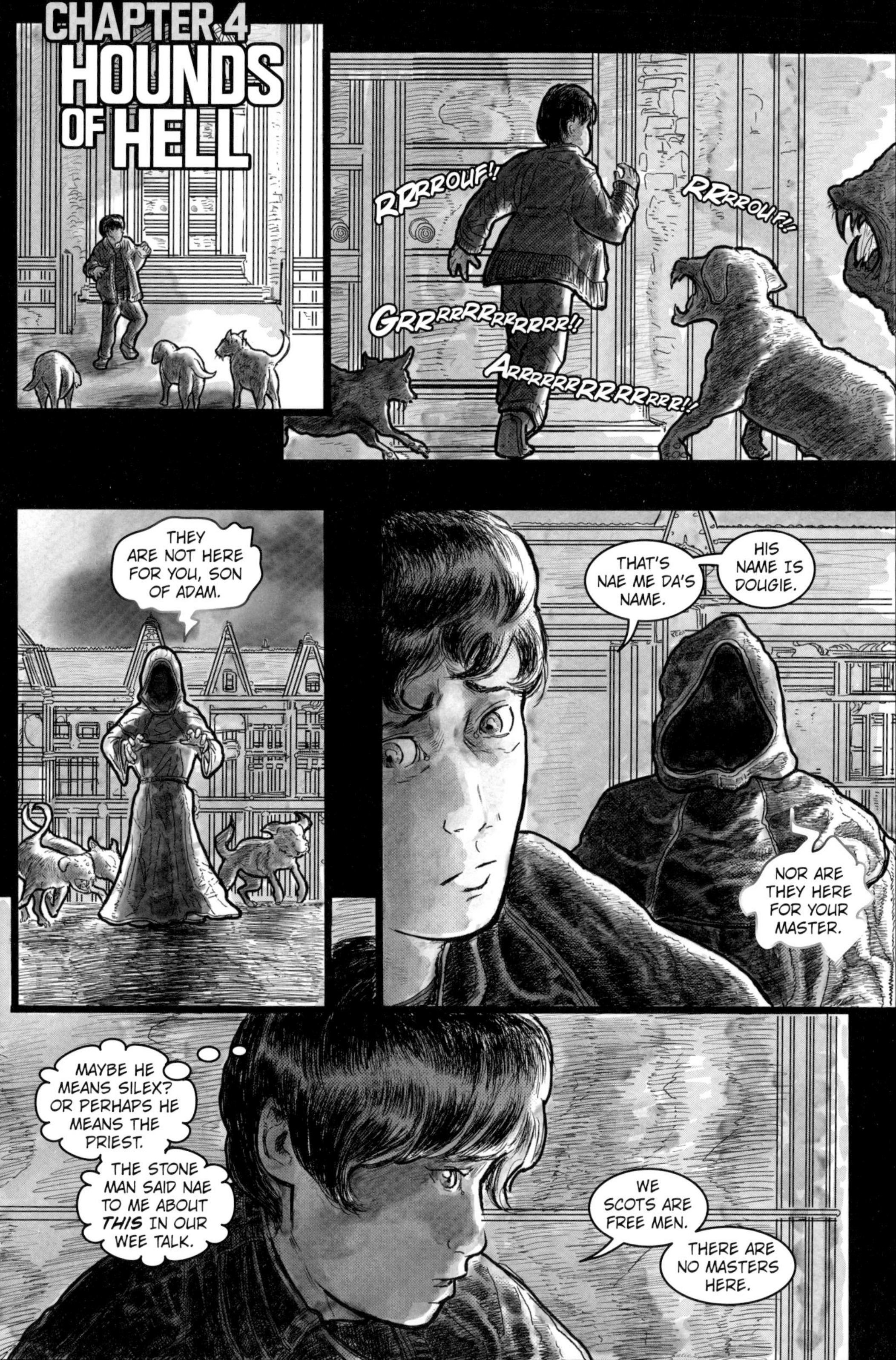
CHAPTER 4
HOUNDS OF HELL
RRRROUF!!
RRRROUF!!
GRRRRRRRRRRRR!!
ARRRRRRRRRRRRR!!
THEY ARE NOT HERE FOR YOU, SON OF ADAM.
THAT'S NAE ME DA'S NAME.
HIS NAME IS DOUGIE.
NOR ARE THEY HERE FOR YOUR MASTER.
MAYBE HE MEANS SILEX? OR PERHAPS HE MEANS THE PRIEST.
THE STONE MAN SAID NAE TO ME ABOUT *THIS* IN OUR WEE TALK.
WE SCOTS ARE FREE MEN.
THERE ARE NO MASTERS HERE.

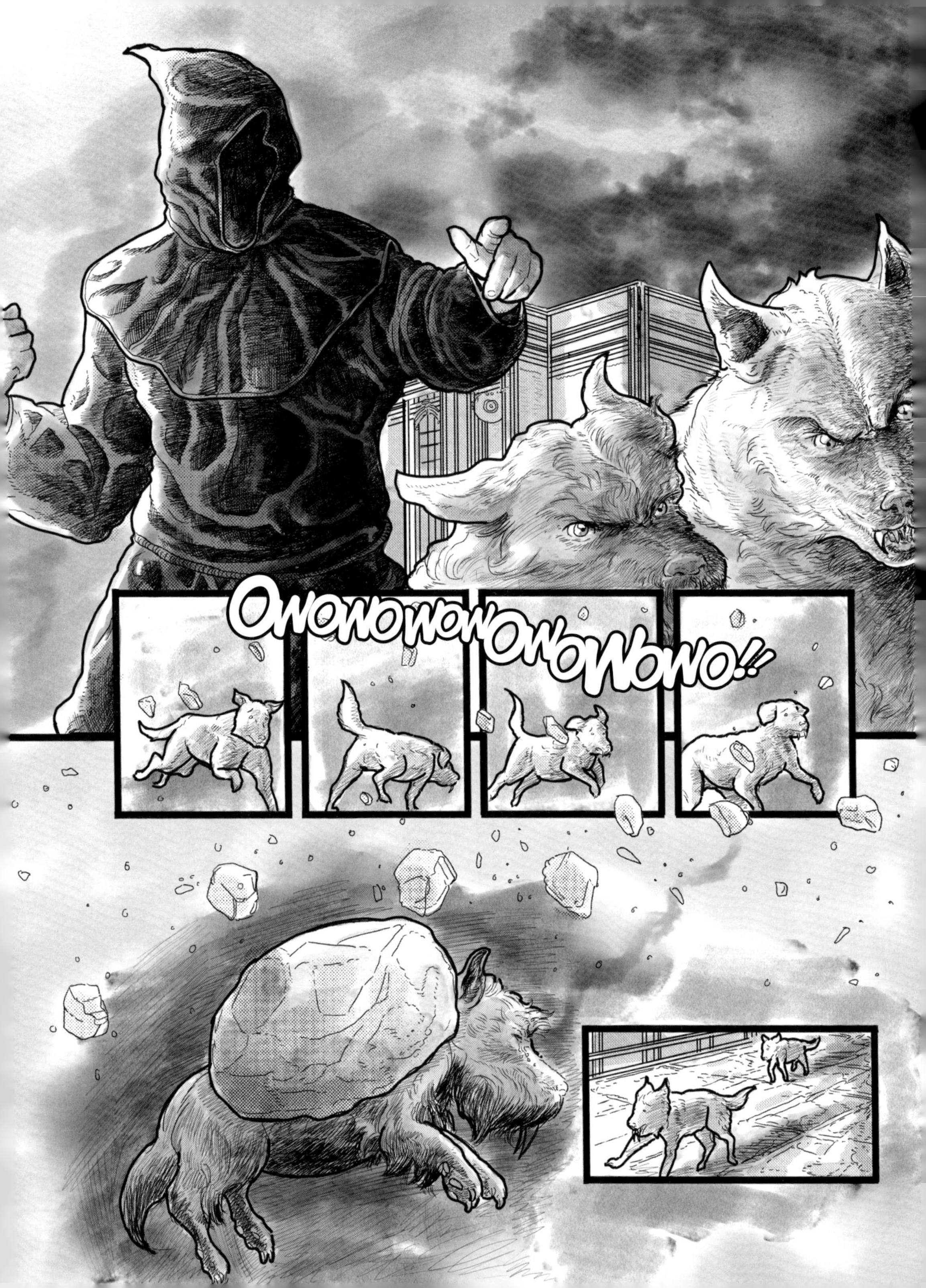
OWOWOWOWOWOWOWOWO!!

AND OF COURSE, WE WILL NOT SEND THE GIRL OUT. OR AT LEAST, NOT YET.

NOT OUT BUT UP.

SHE'S THE ONLY WEE PIECE OF THIS PUZZLE WE'VE GOT HOLD OF.

UP?

BUT SHE'LL BE TOO SCART.

NOT THAT ONE. SHE'S FACED DOWN THE HOUNDS, WON OVER A PRIEST, OUTRUN THE GRIGORI, AND--I'M GUESSING--ESCAPED FROM THE MOUTH OF HELL.

A TALKING STONE MAN WILL BE LIKE A STROLL IN THE GARDEN TO HER.

BRING... HER... *UP*... HERE... TO ...ME.

IS THAT CLEAR ENOUGH? I WILL INTERROGATE HER MYSELF.

GARDEN? OH... YOU MEAN *EDEN*.

PERHAPS I DO.

CHAPTER 6
DANGER LURKS

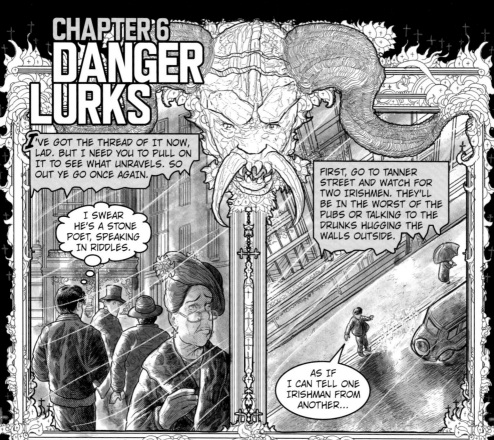

I'VE GOT THE THREAD OF IT NOW, LAD. BUT I NEED YOU TO PULL ON IT TO SEE WHAT UNRAVELS. SO OUT YE GO ONCE AGAIN.

I SWEAR HE'S A STONE POET, SPEAKING IN RIDDLES.

FIRST, GO TO TANNER STREET AND WATCH FOR TWO IRISHMEN. THEY'LL BE IN THE WORST OF THE PUBS OR TALKING TO THE DRUNKS HUGGING THE WALLS OUTSIDE.

AS IF I CAN TELL ONE IRISHMAN FROM ANOTHER...

ONE OF THE IRISHMEN IS ROUND-FACED, INTELLIGENT. FAVORS LONG SIDEBURNS AND WILL PROBABLY DO ALL THE TALKING. THE OTHER HAS AN IDIOT'S EXPRESSION. HE'S THE ONE TO BE DOING ALL THE HITTING.

HOW DOES THE STONE MAN KNOW IT? WTHOUT LEAVNG HIS BLOODY ROOF?

HOW DOES HE GET IT RIGHT EVERY TIME? IT'S NAE HUMAN...

SOUNDS LIKE EVERY PAIR OF IRISHMEN I'VE EVER SEEN.

...WELL, NO ONE CAN ACCUSE HIM OF THAT.

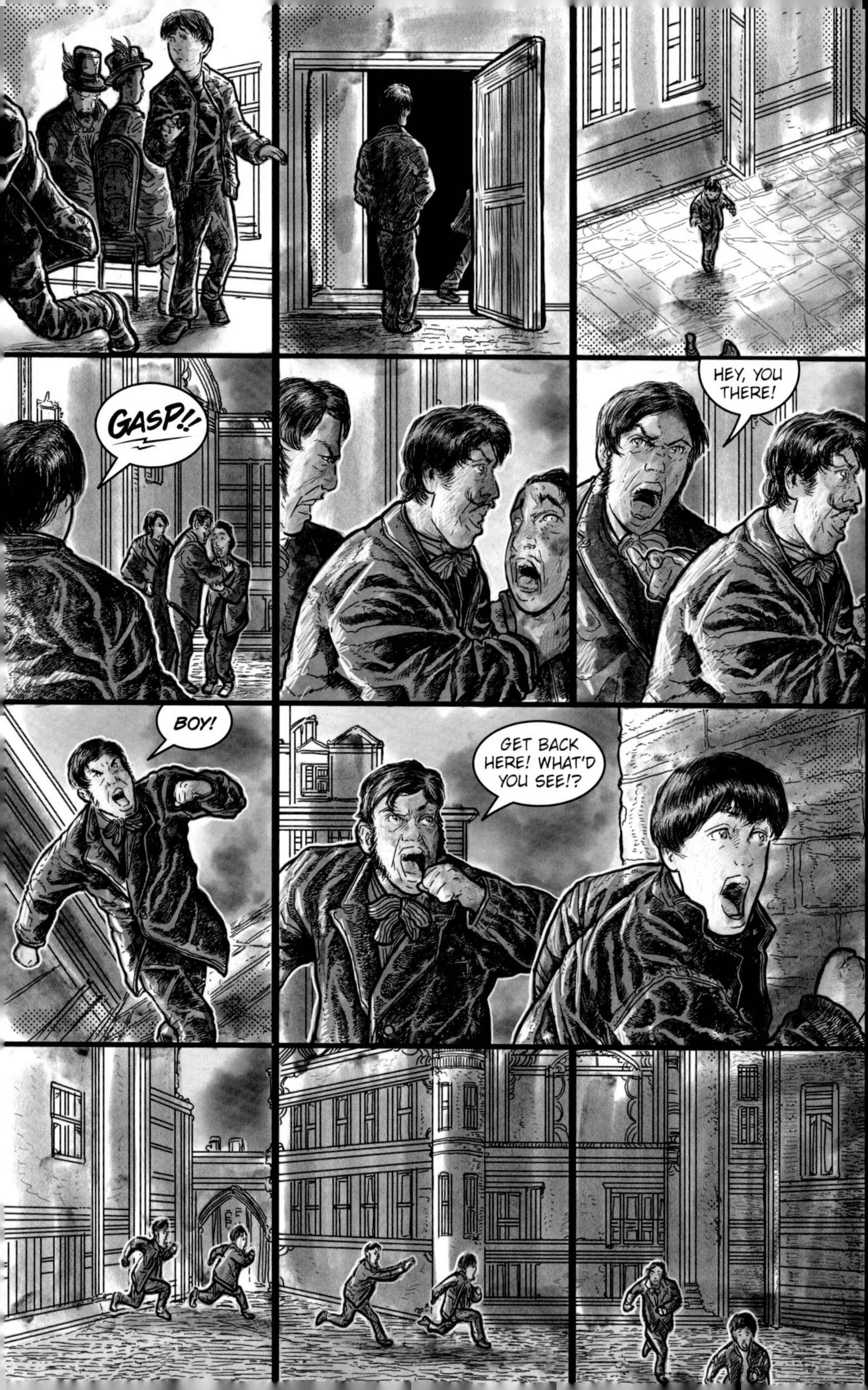
GASP!!
HEY, YOU THERE!
BOY!
GET BACK HERE! WHAT'D YOU SEE!?

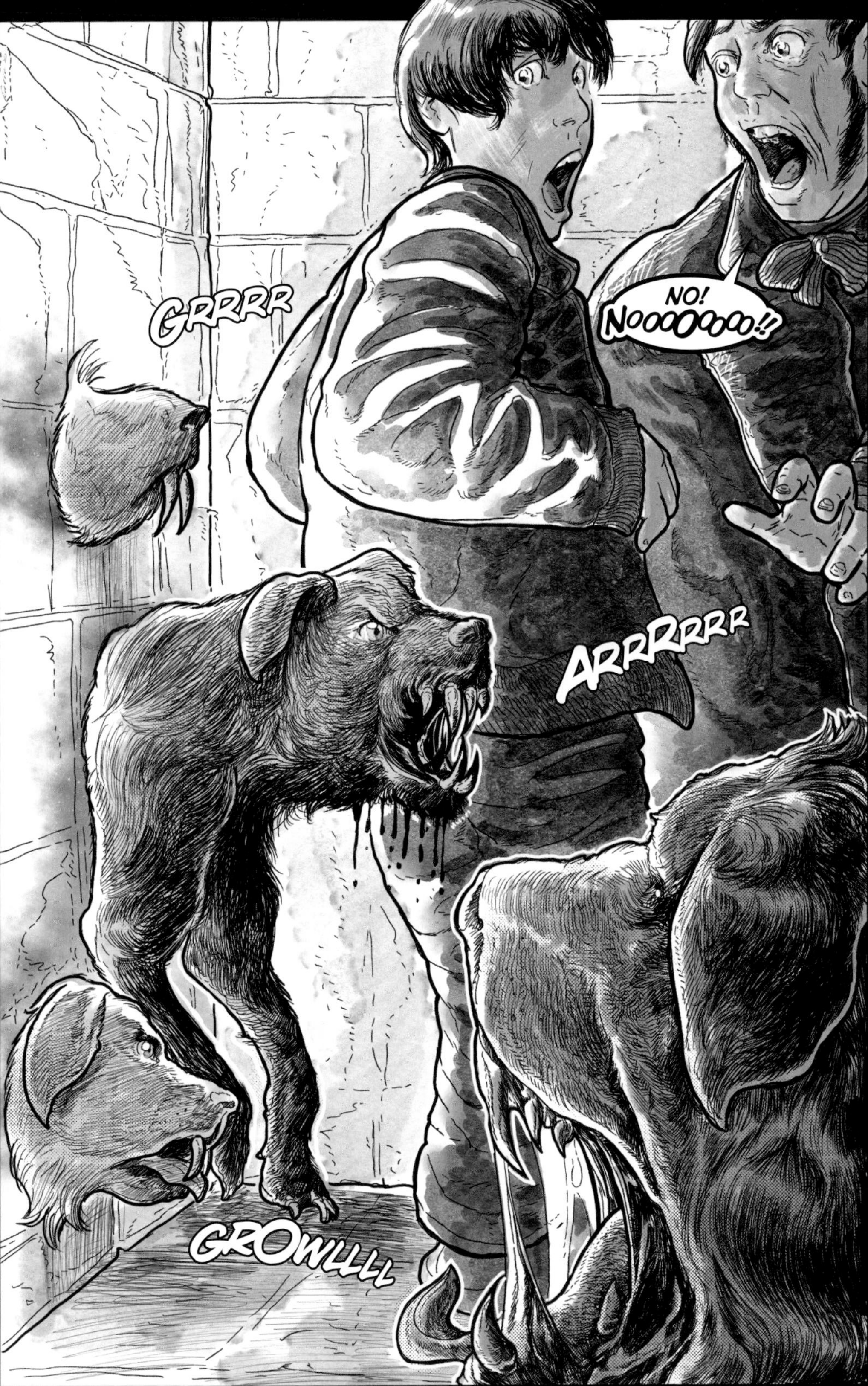
GRRRR
NO! NOOOOOOO!!
ARRRRRR
GROWLLLL

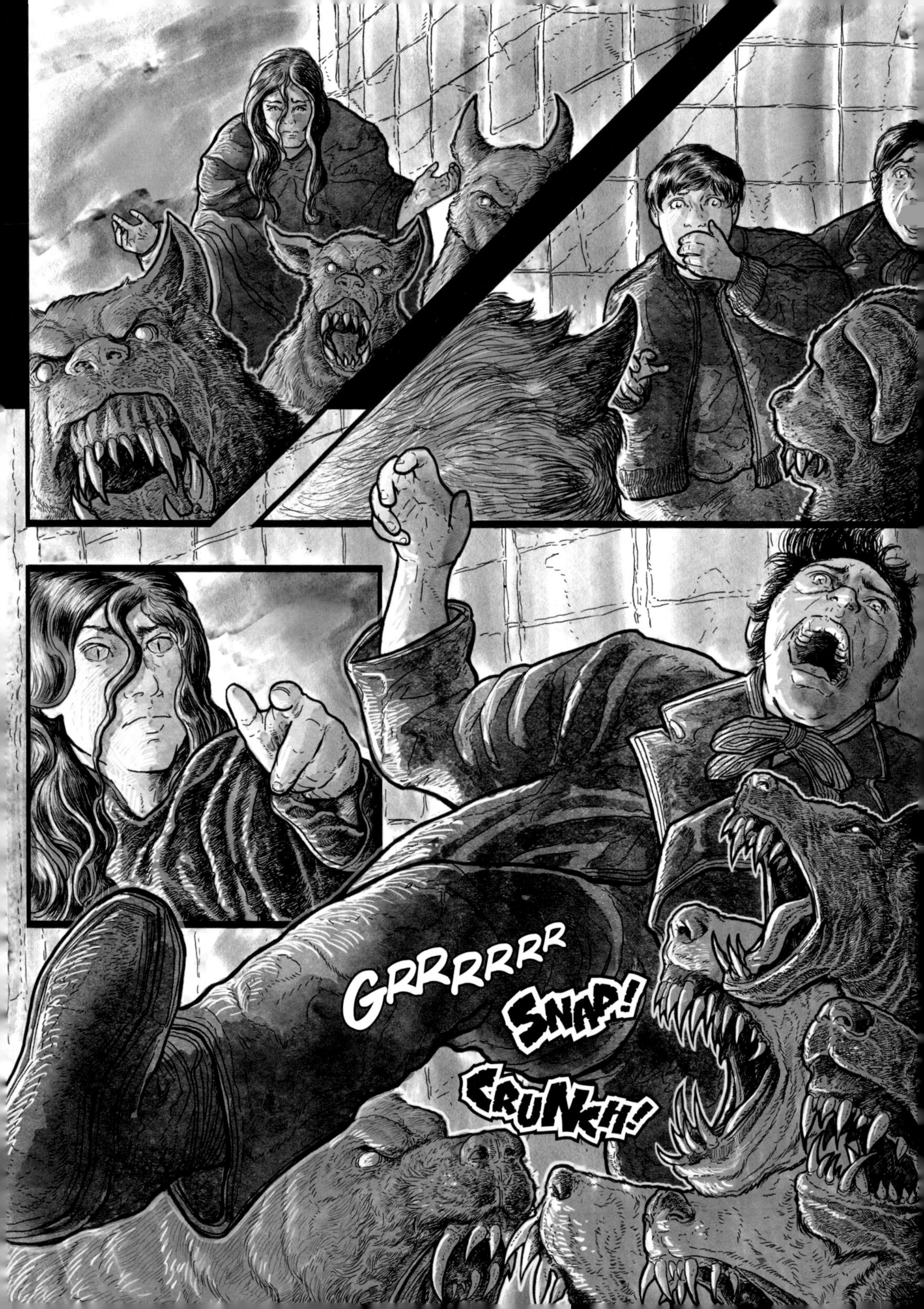
GRRRRRRR
SNAP!
CRUNCH!

CHAPTER 7
HARE TODAY...

huff!
ouff!
OH, GOD, HELP ME...
I'LL NEED THE BELL ROCK LIGHTHOUSE TO GET ME THROUGH THIS.

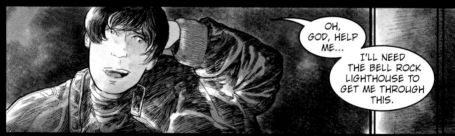

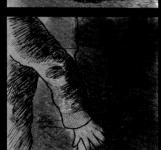

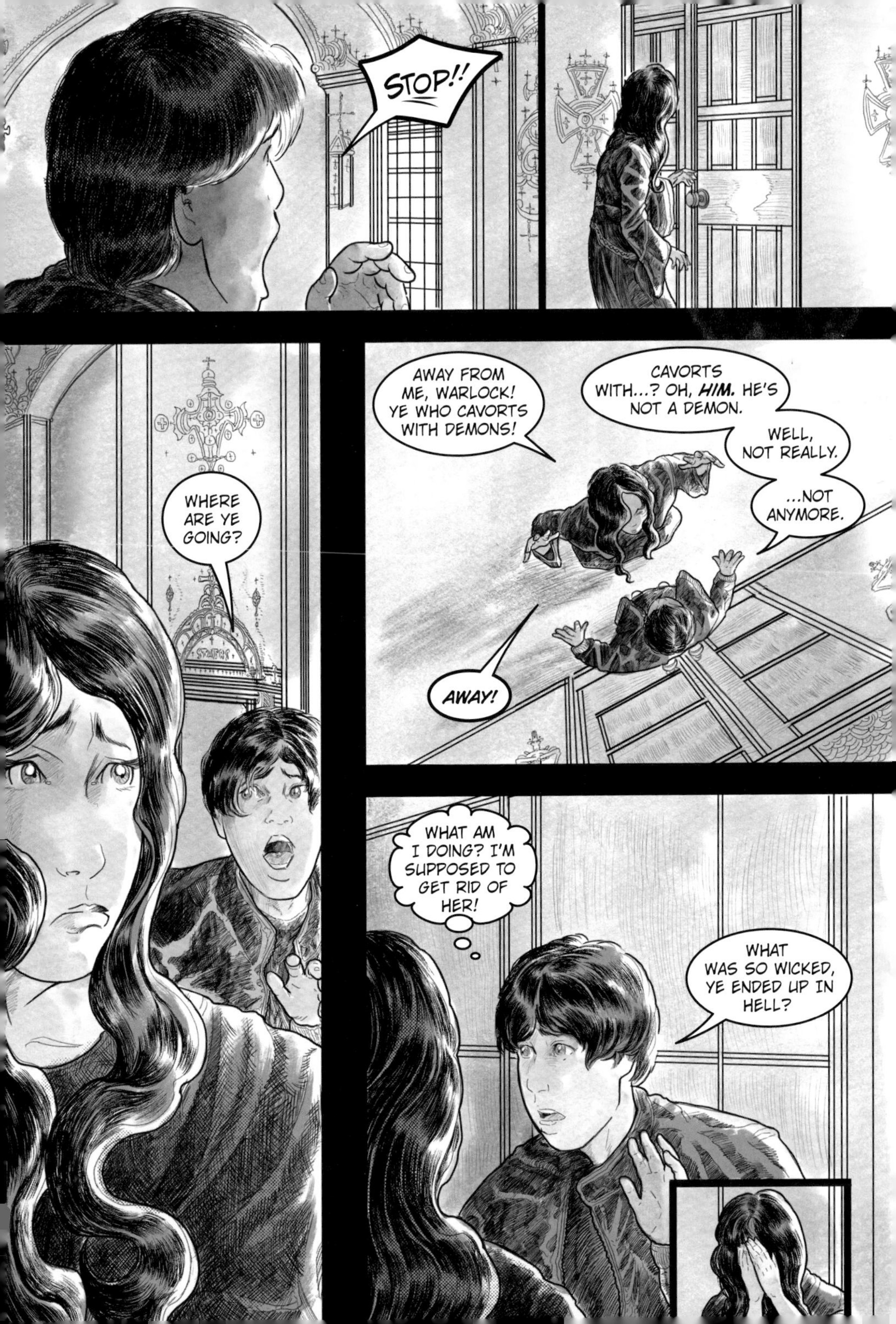
STOP!!
WHERE ARE YE GOING?
AWAY FROM ME, WARLOCK! YE WHO CAVORTS WITH DEMONS!
AWAY!
CAVORTS WITH...? OH, ***HIM.*** HE'S NOT A DEMON.
WELL, NOT REALLY.
...NOT ANYMORE.
WHAT AM I DOING? I'M SUPPOSED TO GET RID OF HER!
WHAT WAS SO WICKED, YE ENDED UP IN HELL?

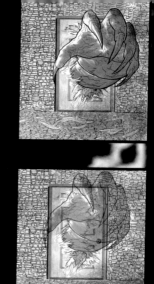

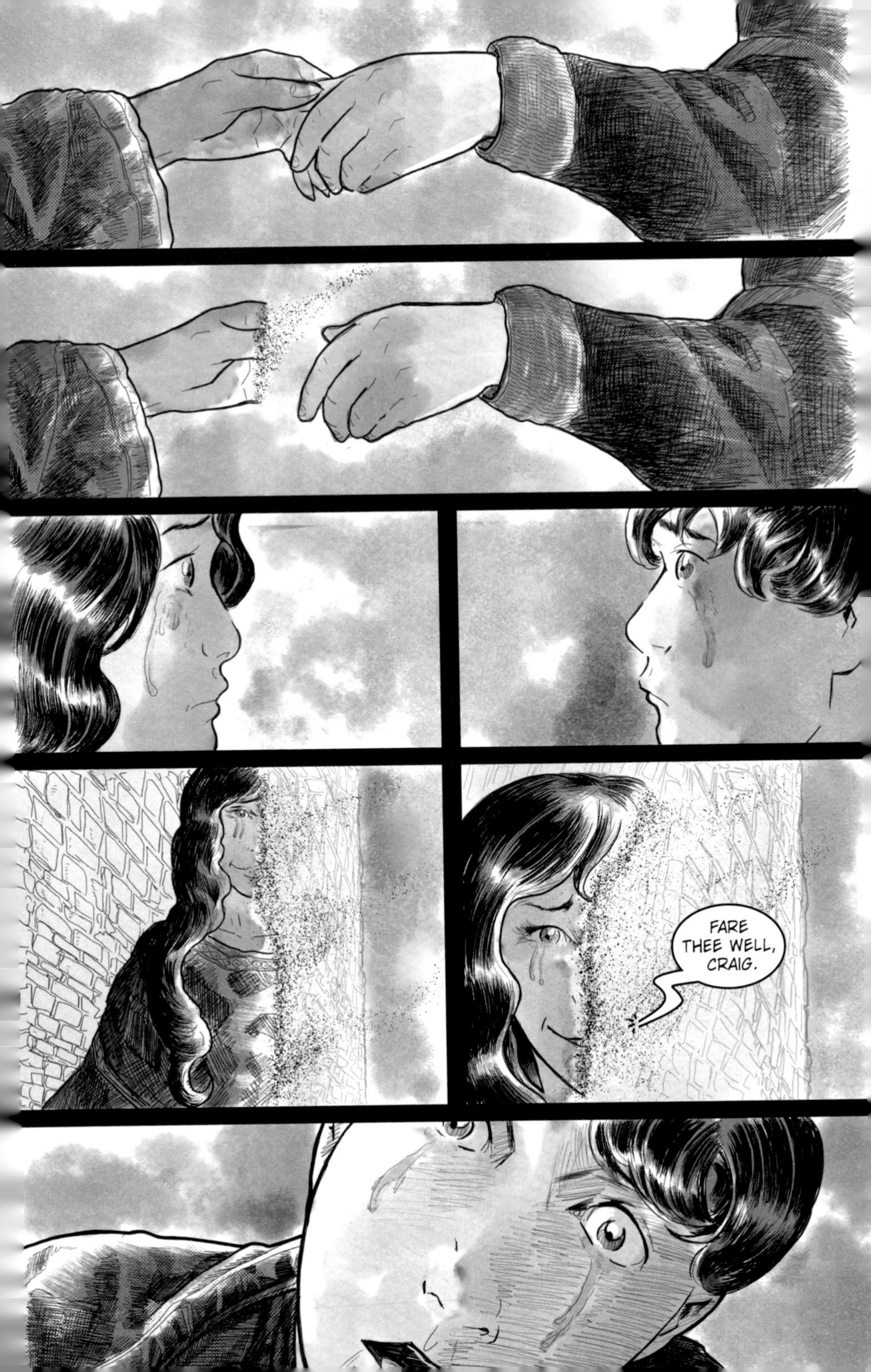
FARE THEE WELL, CRAIG.

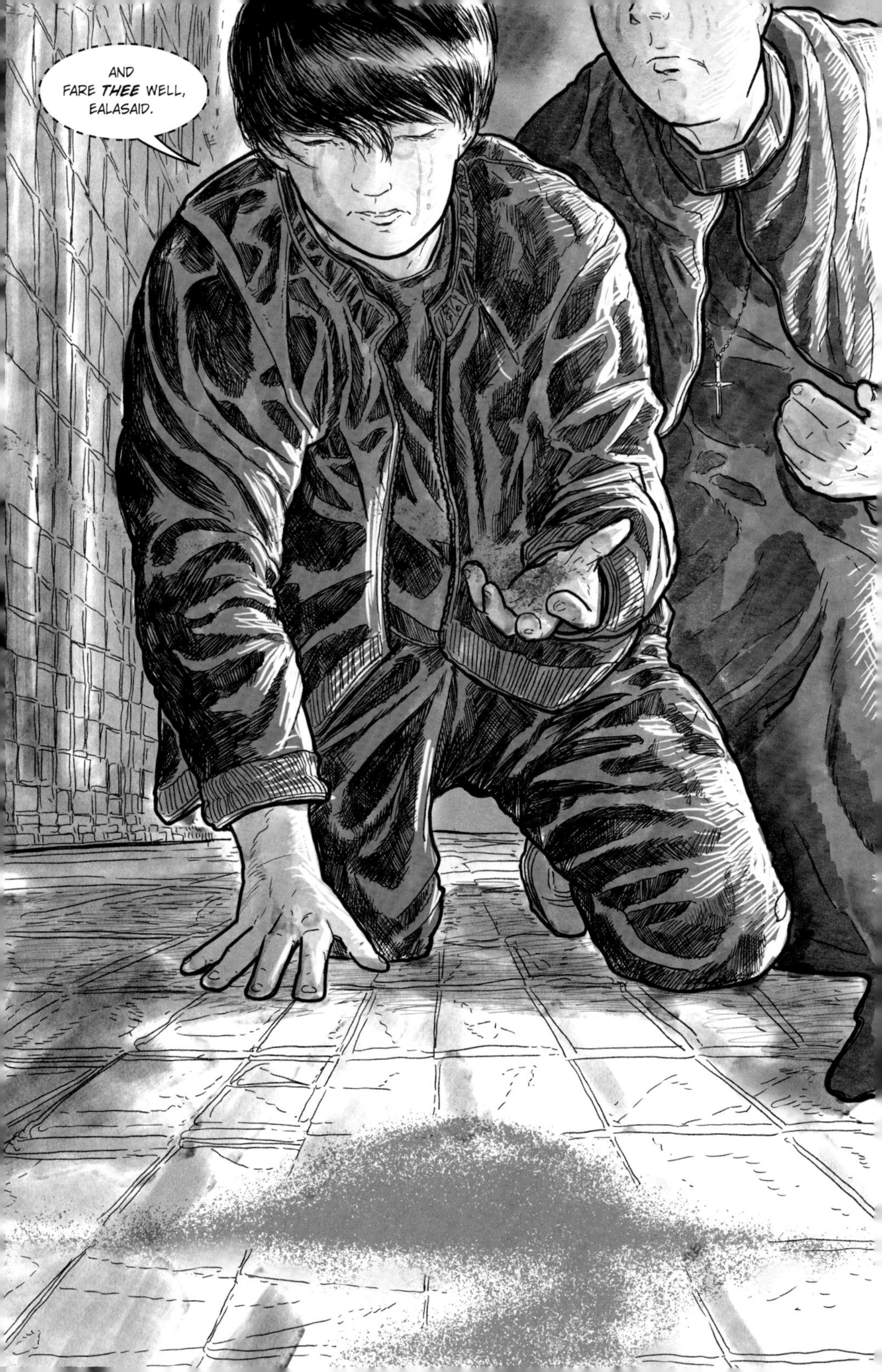
AND FARE THEE WELL, EALASAID.

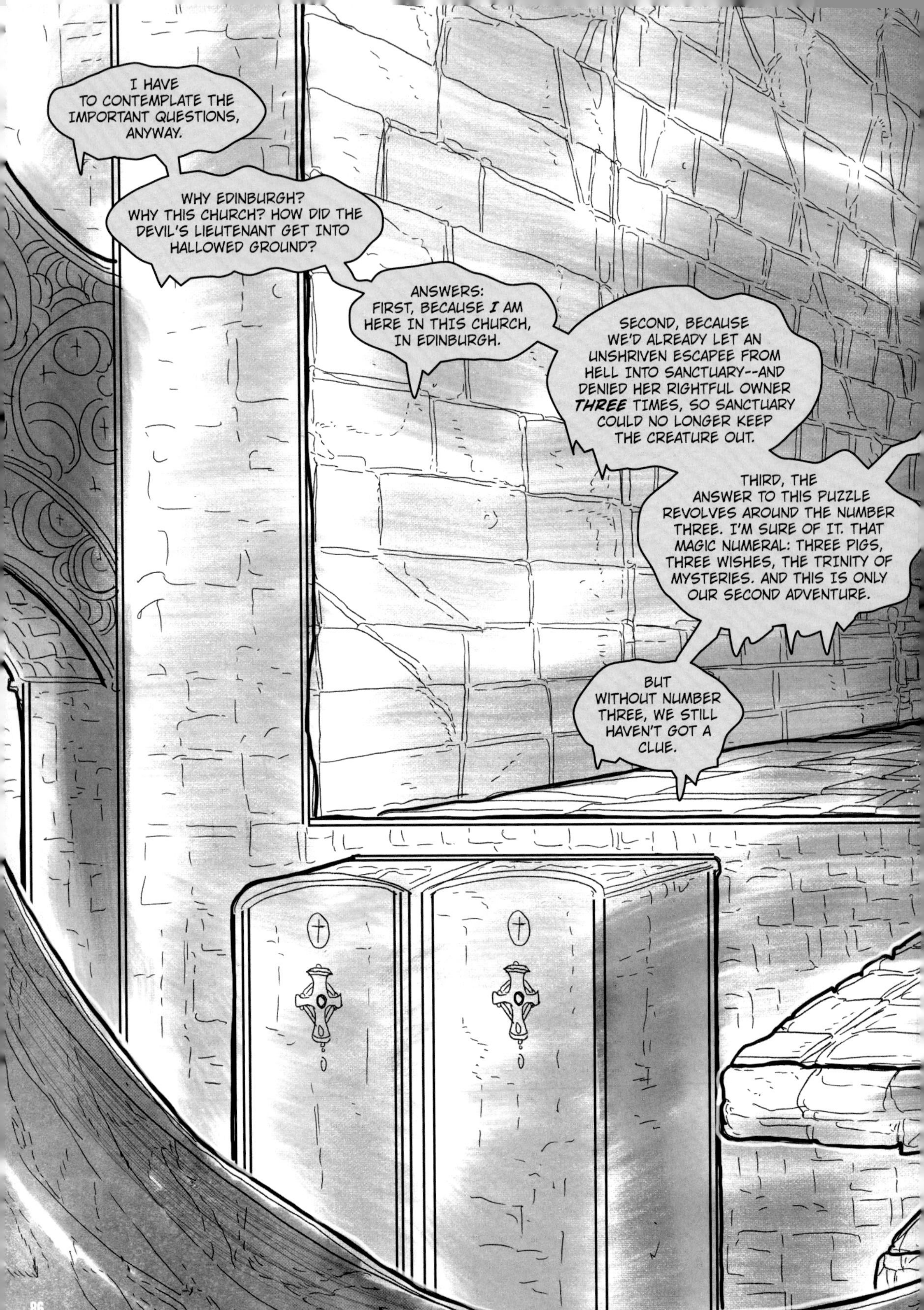
I HAVE TO CONTEMPLATE THE IMPORTANT QUESTIONS, ANYWAY.
WHY EDINBURGH? WHY THIS CHURCH? HOW DID THE DEVIL'S LIEUTENANT GET INTO HALLOWED GROUND?
ANSWERS: FIRST, BECAUSE *I* AM HERE IN THIS CHURCH, IN EDINBURGH.
SECOND, BECAUSE WE'D ALREADY LET AN UNSHRIVEN ESCAPEE FROM HELL INTO SANCTUARY--AND DENIED HER RIGHTFUL OWNER ***THREE*** TIMES, SO SANCTUARY COULD NO LONGER KEEP THE CREATURE OUT.
THIRD, THE ANSWER TO THIS PUZZLE REVOLVES AROUND THE NUMBER THREE. I'M SURE OF IT. THAT MAGIC NUMERAL: THREE PIGS, THREE WISHES, THE TRINITY OF MYSTERIES. AND THIS IS ONLY OUR SECOND ADVENTURE.
BUT WITHOUT NUMBER THREE, WE STILL HAVEN'T GOT A CLUE.